Bronson Howard

Saratoga

Pistols for Seven

Bronson Howard

Saratoga
Pistols for Seven

ISBN/EAN: 9783337343279

Printed in Europe, USA, Canada, Australia, Japan

Cover: Foto ©Andreas Hilbeck / pixelio.de

More available books at **www.hansebooks.com**

SARATOGA;

OR,

"PISTOLS FOR SEVEN."

A Comic Drama

IN FIVE ACTS.

BY

BRONSON HOWARD.

NEW YORK   LONDON
SAMUEL FRENCH   SAMUEL FRENCH
PUBLISHER   PUBLISHER
26 WEST 22D STREET   89 STRAND

COPYRIGHTED

CAST OF CHARACTERS.

	FIFTH AVENUE THEATRE. DEC. 21, 1870.—ORIGINAL.	FIFTH AVENUE THEATRE. JAN. 10, 1874.
MR. ROBERT SACKETT, who loved not wisely but four well,	Mr. JAMES LEWIS.	Mr. JAMES LEWIS.
JACK BENEDICT, a chip of the "regular" sort; in for every-thing "regular,"	Mr. D. H. HARKINS.	Mr. D. H. HARKINS.
PAPA VANDERPOOL, the Parent of the Period,	Mr. DAVIDGE.	Mr. DAVIDGE.
THE HON. WILLIAM CARTER, a relic of the "Old School,"	Mr. WHITING.	Mr. HARDENBERG.
REMINGTON père, travelling for pleasure, and never finding it,	Mr. DE VERE.	Mr. DE VERE.
SIR MORTIMER MUTTONLEG the pride of the Saratoga piazzas	Mr. GEO. PARKES.	Mr. GEO. PARKES.
MR. CORNELIUS WETHERTREE, the "Old Bachelor" of the Period,	Mr. BROWNE.	Mr. WHITING.
MR. LUDDINGTON WHIST, the "Swell" of the "Wells,"	Mr. ARTHUR MATHISON.	Mr. LOUIS JAMES.
FREDERICK AUGUSTUS CARTER, the Youth of the Period,	Mr. BURNETT.	Mr. CONWAY.
FRANK LITTLEFIELD, the Lover of this or any other Period,	Mr. BASCOMB.	Mr. PEAKES.
GYP, the Waiter of the Future, the Present, and the Past,	Mr. BEEKMAN.	Mr. CHAPMAN.
PETE, BELL BOY of the Grand, CLOVER, BELL BOY. DAN, BELL BOY.		G. WASH., BELL BOY.
THE "ARTIST," at the Academy,		Mr. OWEN FAWCETT.
EFFIE REMINGTON, the Belle of the "Union"—the pride of the Saratoga Season—up to "larks," and in for everything "awful," "Clarendon,"	Miss FANNY DAVENPORT.	Miss FANNY DAVENPORT.
LUCY CARTER, the Bride of the Period, and the Pride of the		Miss MINNIE CONWAY.
OLIVIA ALSTON, the Widow of the Period,	Miss CLARA MORRIS.	Miss FANNY MORANT.
VIRGINIA VANDERPOOL, the Pet of the "Union,"	Miss FANNY MORANT.	Miss SARA JEWETT.
MRS. VANDERPOOL, a Mother of the Period,	Miss LINDA DIETZ.	Mrs. GILBERT.
MRS. GAYLOVER, Saratoga knows her well,	Mrs. GILBERT.	Miss MARY NORTON MAFOY.
MUFFINS, an "Exile" of the Period,	Mrs. LIZZIE WINTER.	Miss NELLIE MORTIMER.
LILLY LIVINGSTONE, the Glory of "Marvins,"	Miss AMY AMES.	Miss NINA VARIAN.
AG. OGDEN,	Miss KATE CLAXTON.	Miss STELLA CONGDON.
PUSSY, } Children of Period,	Miss LOUISE VALMER.	Miss ALICE DAILY.
LARKS, }	GERTY NORWOOD.	Miss GERTY.
	Miss KEEN.	

Guests, Promenaders, &c.

SCENERY AND SYNOPSIS.

FIFTH AVENUE THEATRE, Jan. 10, 1874.)

ACT I. The Academy of Design on a Reception Niont (by Duflocq) exhibiting the following rare paintings, by special consent of the artists :

" *Lake Thun*," Switzerland	By J. A. Richards, N.A.
" *Sunset at Sea* "	By E. Morean.
" *Helen of Troy* "	By B. F. Reinhart.
" *Iris* "	From Snedicors.

The Adventure of a "Personal." The white rosebud and the blue rosette. An artistic effort of thirty years demolished.

Two Months.

ACT II.—Congress Springs at Saratoga (by Witham).—Tasting the waters.—A White Mountain Runaway!—and the secret of a dozen warm kisses.

Two Hours.

ACT III.—The Wood near Moon Lake (by Roberts.)—A picnic tableau. [The Scene opens with a Trio, sung by Miss Fanny Davenport, Miss Minnie Conway, and Miss Nina Varian - seconded by Mr. Hart Conway and Mr. J. G. Peakes]. —Hunting Ducks!!! and three claimants for one Bob!

One Hour.

ACT IV.—Parlours at the "Union!"— Coffee and Pistols for Seven!!!

Ten Minutes.

ACT V.—Private Parlour No. 73 (by Witham).—A Mysterious Echo Chamber—with a skeleton in every closet!—A queer entanglement neatly unravelled.

COSTUMES.

First Act. — Full evening or opera dress.
Second Act. — Handsome afternoon or walking dress.
Third Act. — Summer picnic dresses. Ladies in white. Gentlemen in light flannel suits ; straw hats with blue ribbons, &c.
Fourth Act.—Ladies same as in Act Third on first entrance ; all change to rich dinner and evening dresses before second entrance.
Fifth Act.—Same as at end of Fourth Act.

NOTE FOR STAGE MANAGER.

Special Attention should be given to the climax scenes of Act Second and Act Third. These scenes are very effective if properly acted, and very flat if not properly acted. Their effect depends upon the instantaneous response of every actor to his or her cue. If there is a moment's hesitation on the part of any one the interest drops, and it cannot be revived. The phrases, "Go on, Mr. Benedict," &c., in Act Second, should be taken up with great energy and unction by each of the actors in succession. Near the end of Act Third the general movement of all on the stage should be continued with energy, until fall of curtain.

SARATOGA.

ACT I.

SCENE.—*The Academy of Design, New York. Evening reception. The centre gallery. Arches* R. *and* L. *leading to other galleries, in which pictures are seen. Centre door with gallery and pictures beyond. Wide balustrade,* C., *with stairs leading up from below. Pictures on all the walls. Statuary, &c. A landscape on the side up* R. *Nearer front a portrait of a lady, low neck, and a picture to be referred to as the "Card Players." On the left side an easel with a picture representing a white cat, &c., appropriate to* SIR MORTIMER'S *speech about "Nemesis." On an easel,* L. C., *a large painting referred to as the head of Cyrus the Great, and so arranged that* SACKETT *can fall through it.*

Music at rise of curtain. Guests moving to and fro. Gentlemen mostly in evening dress-suit. Ladies in opera costumes. Some looking at pictures with catalogues in their hands. Others passing through entrances R. *and* L. *and* C., *and up and down the stairs. The* ARTIST *with two ladies and a gentleman before the picture on easel* L. C. *The* ARTIST *motioning in dumb show, apparently pointing out its merits in detail. During the conversation he walks out with party,* L., *still talking to them.* OGDEN *with a gentleman pauses up* L., *before the white cat picture,* SIR MORTIMER MUTTONLEGG *standing at her* R. LIVINGSTON *with a gentleman pauses before the landscape up* R., MAJOR LUDDINGTON WHIST *joins her, standing on her* L.

OGDEN (*coming forward with* SIR MORTIMER, L.). No. 395—What is the subject of No. 395, Sir Mortimer ?

SIR MORT. (*looking at catalogue*). A-h—" Nemesis "——by J. H. Dolphe.

OGDEN. Ah ! I was wondering if that was "Nemesis "——
Nemesis is such a sweet pretty subject to illustrate.

SIR MORT. R. Y-e-s, that is—ah—yes—very pretty subject
indeed—a-h—by the-way—what is a " Nemesis," Miss Ogden ? Do you know if the catalogue didn't say this was a
picture of—a-h—"Nemesis "——I should have taken it for
a—cat—watching a—a-h—mouse -and a—chair—and—
a-h—a big piece of cheese on the table.

OGDEN. Why " Nemesis " is the name of the cat, I suppose, Sir Mortimer.

SIR. MORT. Oh—a-h—exactly—I—a-h—never heard the
name before.

    [*The* ARTIST *goes out with party* L. F. *motioning as if
    talking earnestly.*

LIVINGSTON (L). Oh ! what a darling picture—the clouds
are so very delicate—as fleecy—and as light as wool or-—
or cotton, they look so very real.

THE MAJOR (L. C.). They do look *real*—remarkably like
cotton in that respect, Miss Livingston.

LIVINGSTON. And the water is so exactly like real water
—it seems as though you could bathe in that little brook---—
No--it isn't a brook—it's only a stone fence in the fore-
ground.

THE MAJOR. That's a very odd mistake. No gentleman
could make it. I never mistook a stone fence for water in
my life.

LIVINGSTON. No. 273. What is the subject of this one,
Major Whist ?

THE MAJOR (*reading from catalogue*). " A Landscape "
I should almost have expected as much if I hadn't seen the
catalogue—these artists are particularly definite in their
choice of titles.

    [*The* ARTIST *re-enters with a lady and gentleman—
    proceeds to motion before painting as before.*

OGDEN (R. C.). Oh ! Sir Mortimer. You English gentlemen
have travelled so much, and seen so many pictures, you must
favour us with your criticisms as you go along, I do so dote
on English gentle——I mean I do so dote on pictures, Sir
Mortimer.

SIR MORT. (R.). Y-e-s.

OGDEN (*sits* C.). What do you really think of this one, for
instance ? You mustn't be too severe on our American
artists.

SIR MORT. (*looking at picture*) Well—a-h--y-e-s—I- a-h
—strong, decidedly strong ; we can—ah—hardly compare
American artists with Raphael or Michael Angelo—particularly when they are painting—a-h—cats. This picture is

a-h—strong—in its way. I should say that the cat, however, was much stronger than the mouse.

OGDEN (*sits*). Very appropriately so, Sir Mortimer.

SIR MORT. And — a-h — the — ah — cheese — is — a-h — stronger than either.

[*The* ARTIST *walks out* R. E. *with lady and gent, motioning as if speaking earnestly.*

LIVINGSTON. And this one, major ?

THE MAJOR. "A portrait of a lady" (*consulting his catalogue*). Another very definite title—who would have imagined, if we hadn't seen it in print, that this was a portrait of a lady ? I should have mistaken her for the wife of a fortunate Wall Street broker ; and here is the Wall Street broker himself (*motioning to next picture, then reading from his catalogue*). "Gentlemen playing at cards." The "gentleman" who has just played the knave, you see, has won the trick. Refer again, Miss Livingston, to the picture of the broker's wife ; there are diamonds on her breast—how insulted she would be if she were called—a *gambler's* wife ! —*Au revoir*, Miss Livingston.

[*He bows easily and strolls* L., *the* ARTIST *re-enters at this point with two ladies from* R. 1. E. *He proceeds to point out the merits of his pictures in dumb show.*

LIVINGSTON (*meantime to gentleman as the* MAJOR *walks away*). Major Luddington Whist is in one of his bitter moods to-day.—It has been hinted in society that he is a gambler by profession. If that be true, he is sometimes, annoyed, perhaps, that other successful gamblers should secure a more certain footing in society.

THE ARTIST (L. C. *enthusiastically*). This has been the work of my life, Mrs. Turningham. I have spent years upon every detail. It is the head of Cyrus the Great—as you will see, of course, at the first glance. This noble man —— Ah, Miss Livingston ! (*Detaining Livingston, who is running by with a gentleman.*) Delighted to see you this evening, Mr. Alterbury.—One moment, Mrs. Turningham. (*Turning and detaining the lady and gentleman, who had moved as if to leave.*) Your pardon for the interruption. (*To* LIVINGSTON) Delighted to see your respected parents in my studio again—Christian Association building—do not misunderstand me—we artists merely occupy studios in the building—we have no other personal association with Christians. I was calling Mrs. Turningham's attention to the last finished product of my easel. This has been the work of my life, ladies. I have spent years upon every detail ; it is the head of Cyrus the Great, as you see, of course,

at a glance. This noble man—— Ah, Miss Ogden! (*To*
OGDEN, *who has walked down* L. *with a gentleman.* SIR MORT.
*strolls across up stage and looks at pictures, moving quietly
down* L. *The* MAJOR, *looking at pictures* R., *moving gra-
dually up.*)—Delighted to see you, Miss Ogden ; mamma
well? I was calling the ladies' attention to the last finished
product of my easel. This has been the work of my life,
Miss Ogden. I have spent years upon every detail—it is
the head of Cyrus the Great, as you see, of course, at a
glance. This noble man——

OGDEN (*looking at the picture on other easel*, R. C.). What
is the subject of this one, Mr. Langdon—No. 78?

THE ARTIST. That—a-h—a young artist—promising—but
crude as yet—thin in colour—and he needs experience in
drawing. As I was about to remark—may I call your attention, by-the-way, to a little touch of colour *here?*—that
nose was the labour of months. (*As he goes on, the various
couples walk away in different directions, strolling up and off
at their leisure. The* ARTIST *proceeds, intent on his picture,
pointing out each feature with his finger.*)—You notice the
curl of the lip ; I studied that from an old Egyptian relic—
there are weeks of study in the curl of that lip—pride—royal
dignity—military precision--a touch of cruelty. The inner
corners of the eyes, too : do you see the world of meaning
in the inner corner of that eye—the left eye, particularly?
Could any one fail to recognize that left eye for the left eye
of Cyrus the Great? You will excuse the enthusiasm of an
artist—but this particular head is the crowning effort of my
artistic life. Notice, if you please, the curl of the ear—do
you not agree with me, that there is something peculiarly
—— (*Discovers that he is alone and talking to himself; looks
R. and* L. *indignantly, and marches out* R. 1. E.)

SIR MORT. (*staring out* R. 1. E.). That is a particularly
charming young girl with her papa, in front of the picture
of Diana at the bath—charming girl.

THE MAJOR (*coming down* L.). Sir Mortimer Muttonlegg !

SIR MORT. Major Luddington Whist : at your *service,
my dear major.

THE MAJOR. What do you think of our American art,
Sir Mortimer?

SIR MORT. I—I think—y-e-s—a-h—that is—a-h—very
nice painting in America. (*Aside, looking out* R.) That girl
has an exquisite complexion! (*Aloud, to* MAJOR.) Some
very nice painting in America (*advancing*).

THE MAJOR. Speaking of art, Sir Mortimer— What do
you think of our American ladies?

SIR MORT. Well—a-h—I don't profess to be much of an art-

critic, my dear major ; but, a-h—in regard to your American
ladies, I—a-h—the fact is—I've only been in America three
weeks, and your American girls are the most unaccountable
creatures. We English gentlemen can't understand them at
all, you know. By-the-way, you don't happen to know the
young lady standing before the picture of Diana at the Bath
—with an elderly gentleman?

THE MAJOR. Oh! but I do though—one of the greatest
belles in the city, Miss Effie Remington. Rich, piquant, wild
as a young hawk, an heiress too; half the fellows in New
York are in love with her. (*Looking off* L.) Ah! and there
is Miss Virginia Vanderpool—another of our belles—with
Mr. Cornelius Wethertree—the elderly bachelor—who has
made love to every marriageable young lady within his
reach for the last thirty years or more.

SIR MORT. She's a deucedly charming girl! isn't she,
major? A deucedly charming girl.

THE MAJOR. The Vanderpool you mean? Yes, a devilish
fine girl, my dear Sir Mortimer, but very expensive tastes;
she declines to ride behind anything less than three minutes
on the road. It will pay the lucky one among her admirers
in the end, however—her father owns half a dozen railr ads,
and a branch of National Banks. I've shuffled the cards in
that direction myself. I think it will pay in the end.

SIR MORT. But I was speaking of the other, my dear
major—I referred to the Remington. Charming girl.

THE MAJOR. Charming! yes. Her father is nearly as
rich as Papa Vanderpool himself.

SIR MORT. But seriously I referred to the young lady's
personal charms.

THE MAJOR. And so did I. Old Remington is worth
more than half a million—his daughter Effie is his only
child—could anybody's charms be more "personal" than
that?

[*They walk up. The* MAJOR *afterwards strolls out at his
leisure.*

Enter VIRGINIA VANDERPOOL *and* WETHERTREE, L. 1. E.

WETHERTREE. The picture of "Cupid sharpening his
Arrows" is in the west room, Miss Vanderpool—a very pain-
ful subject to me, however, Miss Virginia—especially when
one of his arrows is at this moment—

VIRGINIA. Ah! Mr. Wethertree, you know how to make
such delightful speeches.

Enter MRS. ALSTON, R. 1. E.

MRS. A. Ah! Virginia, my love.

VIRGINIA. My dear Olivia. (*They meet and kiss.*)

WETHERTREE (*getting* R.). Upon my word, ladies, I envy
you both, I do upon my life.   1—3

VIRGINIA (L.). Oh, you naughty man. I was only just telling him, Mrs. Alston, that he knew so well how to make those delightful speeches.

MRS. A. (C.). I have frequently noticed it myself.

WETHERTREE (*bowing*). You flatter me, ladies.

MRS. A. How could it be otherwise with so many long years of experience?

WETHERTREE. A-h-e-m (*turning away*).

MRS. A. Ah! Sir Mortimer Muttonlegg. *Sir Mort. is passing down* L. Miss Virginia Vanderpool—Sir Mortimer.

SIR MORT. (L.). Ladies!

MRS. A. (C.). Mr. Cornelius Wethertree studying American art and American society at the same time, my dear Sir Mortimer.

SIR MORT. Y-e-s—I—a-h—find it a very agreeable—a-h combination—in fact—I—a-h—by-the-way, Mrs. Alston, you are a—very beautiful—a-h—combination of nature and art yourself. [*She bows to him.*

WETHERTREE (R.). And it would require a very acute observer of both nature and art, madam, to discover where one leaves off and the other begins—ha! ha! ha!

MRS. A. (*after bowing to Wethertree*). Really, gentlemen—you are so very complimentary—allow me to return the compliment, Sir Mortimer, though art, perhaps, deserves the greater share of credit. As for yourself, Mr. Wethertree, nature asserts herself so strongly there—she is fast crowding art aside.

WETHERTREE. Ahem! [WETH. *turns up* R. SIR MORT. L.

MRS. A. Virginia, love, have you decided where to spend the summer yet?

VIRGINIA. We are going to Saratoga.

MRS. A. Delightful, my dear, I am going to the Springs also.

VIRGINIA. Father says we shan't, but that doesn't make any difference, you know.

Enter EFFIE, R. 1. E. *looking cautiously* R. *and* L.

MRS. A. Of course not, my dear. Poor dear Alston! he used to be so determined not to go to Long Branch or Saratoga. There isn't half the interest in going now that I am a widow, and can do as I please.

SIR MORT. (*looking at* EFFIE). Deuced fine girl.

WETHERTREE (*also looking at her*). That is a magnificent creature.

MRS. A. (*seeing Effie*). Why Effie dear.

EFFIE. Eh—oh—how you startled me, Alston. (*Kisses her.*) Vanderpool, my dear. (*Kisses her.*)

WETHERTREE. I shouldn't mind being in Mrs. Alston's place.

SIR MORT. (*up stage*). I—a-h—rather envy Miss Vanderpool.
MRS. A. Not alone, my dear Effie, at the reception.
Where is your papa?
EFFIE. I left father discussing the question of pre-Raphaelite art. whatever that may be, with another old gentleman that knows as little about the subject as papa does.
H-s-h— (*Putting her hands to her lips mysteriously, then taking them by the wrists and moving forward.*) H-s-h, I'm on a lark to-night.
MRS. A. A lark?
VIRGINIA. What's the fun now?
EFFIE. H-s-h, it's an awful lark. I wouldn't tell you what it is for the world; there will be a row if papa finds it out.
VIRGINIA. Yes. Oh! that's real jolly; but won't you tell us?
EFFIE. Not now, perhaps I will some other time, ha—ha—ha! Oh, but it's an *awful* lark. I say, girls, have you made up your mind where you're going to spend the summer? I'm going to Saratoga.
VIRGINIA. Isn't that splendid, Alston? So are we.
EFFIE. Ha—ha—that'll be jolly. Father says I sha'n't go to Saratoga, but I'm getting ready all the same, and when the time comes I'll pat him under the chin, and I'll put my arms around his neck, and I'll pinch his cheeks, and every time he goes to say "No," I'll put my lips over his mouth, and I shan't let him open his lips until he says "Yes."
WETHERTREE *and* SIR MORT. *come down* R. *and* L.
WETHERTREE (L.) and SIR MORT. (R.). Ahem! A-h-e-m.
MRS. A. Sir Mortimer Muttonlegg—Miss Effie Remington.
VIRGINIA. Mr. Cornelius Wethertree. [*They bow very low.*
WETHERTREE. Delighted to make your acquaintance, Miss Remington.
SIR MORT. (R.). Positively charmed to meet you, Miss Remington.
WETH. I assure, Miss Remington, that nothing——
SIR MORT. Nothing could possibly ——
WETH. and SIR MORT. I——
[*They approach* C. *until their heads meet in front of* EFFIE, *they look at each other and then turn up stage indignantly.*
MRS. A. Ha—ha. A double conquest, Effie.
VIRGINIA. Two birds with one shot.
EFFIE. Down on both alleys.
MRS. A. Tell me, Effie; with all your little conquests and your flirtations, is there no one yet—with a moustache, for instance, and with fascinating manners, you know,—is there no one that calls for a genuine sigh now and then?

EFFIE. Heigho! Y-e-s, he *has* got a moustache.

MRS. A. and VIRG. Ha—ha—ha.

EFFIE. Isn't there some one, Alston, that *you* are particularly partial to?

MRS. A. Well, I'm a woman, and we women must be petted, you know. How is it with Virginia?

VIRGINIA. Heigho, I am a woman too, I suppose.

EFFIE. I once thought I never should care for one man more than another, men are all so stupid after you know them. But when Robert——

MRS. A. Robert!

VIRGINIA. Robert! why that is the name of my—(*checks herself*).

MRS. A. How very odd ; mine is named Robert also.

EFFIE. Yours Robert, and yours ; why isn't it funny? What's his last name, Virginia?

VIRGINIA. Oh! that's a secret.

EFFIE. A secret. That's real nice ; tell us all about it.

VIRGINIA. But it's a real secret! What's your Robert's last name?

EFFIE. That's a secret, too.

VIRGINIA. Yes ; tell us all about it.

EFFIE. Oh, but it's a real secret. Olivia, what's the last name of your Robert?

MRS. A. (R.C.). If you young girls can keep a real secret, surely a widow can be equally profound. But what an odd fancy, Effie,—a rosette upon your shoulder.

EFFIE. Do you think it pretty? It's only a fancy of mine for to-night. I say Vanderpool! Alston! don't let these fellows stay around me ; I have other business to attend to now ; take 'em with you when you go.

MRS. A. My dear Sir Mortimer, I was looking for Bierstadt's picture in the East Room, will you join me?

SIR MORT. (R.). Certainly—a-h—only too happy, of course. (*Aside.*) Confoundedly awkward. I began to hope we should be left alone.   [MRS. A. *takes his arm.*

VIRGINIA. You were going to show me the picture of Cupid and his arrows, in the West Room, Mr. Wethertree?

WETH. Certainly: I—ah!—(*aside*)—I wish Cupid and his arrows were shot.

     [WETH. *and* VIRG. *go* R., MRS. A. *and* SIR. M. *go* L.

WETH. Good-afternoon, Miss Remington.

SIR MORT. *Au revoir*, Miss Remington.

[*Both going. They see handkerchief which* EFFIE *drops. Both gentlemen run to pick it up.* SIR MORT. *gets it. Then* EFFIE *drops her fan, which* WETHERTREE *picks up ; they both bow. Meet each other* C. ; *as before, draw up indignantly. Return to their ladies, and exeunt* R. *and* L., *leaving* EFFIE *alone.*

EFFIE (*alone*). Now for my lark: he was to have on a white rose-bud, tied with a white ribbon. Let me see— (*looks at watch*)—oh! it's fifteen minutes yet. I was to have the rosette—(*arranging it*): that's right. I wonder what sort o' looking man he is. I know what I'll do: I'll keep my hand over the rosette, and if I don't like his looks, when I see the rose-bud, I'll steal away and I'll take off the rosette, and he will never know that any one was here to see him at all!—Ha, ha, ha! (*Going* L. 1.E. LADIES *and* GENTLEMEN *cross as she is going out* L. *She stares at the* GENTLEMEN'S *lapelles. When they look in return, she draws up with dignity, and passes* L.) Oh, but it's an awful lark!
[*Exit* L. *arch.*

Enter BENEDICT, *followed by* ROBERT SACKETT, *upstairs.*

BEN. Hold on, Bob. What the deuce! Fifteen minutes of nine; exactly fifteen minutes a-head of time: that's not what I call punctuality. Punctuality is on time exactly to the minute. Five minutes after time, a broken engagement. Fifteen minutes a-head of time, a quarter of an hour lost. Punctuality neither loses time nor keeps an appointment waiting. Regularity, my dear Sackett, absolutely, regularity should be the rule of every man's life. Regularity has been the rule of my life; I am a success. Regularity is the rule of nature. Nature is a success. But this appointment of yours at nine o'clock. You haven't told me as yet what the nature of the appointment is. Whom are you to meet? A hundred to one it's a woman. You have been as glum all the afternoon as if you had just buried your first wife, and the lady you had chosen for your second was about to marry another man.

SACK. My dear Benedict, if you love me, don't trifle with a subject so sacred as that of matrimony. Wedlock! Two souls in the fond embrace of everlasting love? Two hearts that beat eternally in unison—two——

BEN. Two mouths to feed, two sets of limbs to clothe, too much, too long, too many children, too two fools——

SACK. You don't appreciate the sublimity of love.

BEN. Oh! certainly I do. The sublimity of love is the regular thing at our age. I was in love myself once, sublimity and all. It is, without exception, the most disagreeable memory of my life; I couldn't be regular in anything, except my meals. Why, I actually forgot to wind my watch three mornings in succession.

SACK. You say you were in love; you didn't marry the girl, it seems.

BEN. Being a bachelor still, I certainly did not. The lady jilted me, and married another gentleman. She did better, however, than if she had married me. Her husband died in less than three years—I didn't. She is now a dashing widow, the envy of her own sex and the admiration of ours.

SACK. Ah! Benedict—Benedict, it is plain you have never loved as I love.

BEN. No; I dare say I haven't.

SACK. I am an utterly wretched individual; the fact is, I'm in a quandary.

BEN. M——, m——. The lady who has secured your affections does not return your love?

SACK. She adores me. We are engaged to be married.

BEN. (R.). She is poor, perhaps; what of that? You have an income.

SACK. Her father has retired from Wall Street, with six or eight railroads in his vest pocket.

BEN. Her parents object to the match?

SACK. Her parents never saw me, and they haven't the slightest idea that I'm engaged to their daughter.

BEN. Ah, I see; the time has come for you to declare your love, and you are in suspense as to the result?

SACK. Quite the contrary. I'm not in the least suspense.

BEN. Well, but if you really love the girl ——

SACK. Really love her! Never man loved woman before as I love Virginia. Her name is Virginia; beautiful name, isn't it?

BEN. Very well, my dear fellow; if you love the girl ——

SACK. My dear Benedict, please don't say "if I love the girl." My love is as fixed as the fixed stars themselves: please don't say, "If I love the girl."

BEN. Well, you love the girl—the girl loves you—you feel no misgivings about the final result. I cannot see where the difficulty lies; you said you were in a quandary!

SACK. Y-e-s, so I am. The fact is, Jack, I'm engaged to another girl also. (BENEDICT starts). I know it isn't quite regular, Jack; but it's true.

BEN. (after a pause). M—, m—, that is awkward. However, if you have been imprudent, my dear Bob, the manly, regular course is to acknowledge your error as soon as possible. Say to the other girl, at once, that you do not love her—and——

SACK. Not love her, my dear Jack! I love Effie devotedly —her name is Effie. I adore the very earth she steps upon. Not love my Effie! Ah! Benedict, Benedict, it is evident you have never loved as I love.

BEN. No! egad I haven't; one woman at a time was enough for me.

SACK. We're engaged to be married. Her father is an elderly brute ; being a father, of course he couldn t be any thing but a brute. He's a gruff old coon, a rich old widower. he has never permitted my acquaintance, nor tolerated my advances. He is more jealous of his daughter than of his gold. But Effie and I see each other two or three times a week, and we are as happy as ever two young lovers were in the world.

BEN. Of course, then, now that you and Effie are so happy, you'll speak to Virginia like a man, and say that you've ceased to love her, and——

SACK. Ceased to love Virginia ! My dear Benedict, I love Virginia from the bottom of my heart.

BEN. Oh ! very well, then, you will say to Effie that you have ceased to love her, and——

SACK. Ceased to love Effie ! Have I not already told you that I adore the very earth she steps upon.

BEN. Then Virginia must be——

SACK. Virginia ! Sweet syllables ! They run through my brain continually.

BEN. (*decidedly*). Then certainly Effie must be——

SACK. Effie ! That darling name ! I can't get it out of my head —

BEN. Why, hang it, man ! you can't love both girls at once.

SACK. I don't. I never think of them both at the same time. And—a-h—Benedict—that isn't all.

BEN. That isn't all ! Another woman ?

SACK. A widow.

BEN. A widow !—the devil !

SACK. Exactly ! An admirable creature ; dashing, brilliant, voluptuous. We are engaged to be married.

BEN. Engaged to be married ?

SACK. Yes ; but I give you my word, Jack, I never intended it ; it was an accident.

BEN. An accident ?

SACK. Purely an accident ; I never could imagine how it happened ! One night I had been sitting alone with the widow in the conservatory ; my arm was about her waist, you know, and all that sort of thing. What the deuce I had been saying to her I never could recollect. But the widow suddenly informed me that she accepted my proposal, and was mine for ever.

BEN. She was yours for ever ?

SACK. She was mine for ever ; imagine my astonishment, if you please. She was my widow for ever. I made the best of my situation, of course, and as a matter of courtesy, I sent her an engagement present next day I proposed to Effie, Jack, because I couldn't help it. I felt an irresistible impulse, from the moment I saw her, to make that particular woman my wife. As to Virginia, we melted together as it were—we fused. She is a tender, delicate, delicious little creature. But the widow was an accident—a magnificent woman—all that a man could wish—and more too; —but an accident. Jack, purely an accident.

BEN. And what do you propose to do about it, Bob?

SACK. Do? Why, nothing for the present. I intend to fly from my lovely persecutors, and lead the life of an anchorite and a hermit—at Saratoga.

BEN. Saratoga! Excellent! an admirable place for an anchorite. I intend to go there myself.

SACK. You do? All right, we'll go together. I'll drown my sorrows in Congress-water and dissipation; with three months to think about it, perhaps I can get out of my dilemma. But, by-the-way, it is time for my appointment. (*Looks* R. *and* L.)

BEN. Another woman in that, I suppose.

SACK. No; only "a butterfly,"—ha—ha—ha! (*takes piece of newspaper out of his pocket*). Read that, Benedict. (*Gives it to him.*)

BEN. (*reading*). "X.Y.Z., or any other man. Which of you wishes to correspond with an angel warranted genuine; just imported. Only real article in the market. No widowers need apply. N.B.—Highest price paid for cast-off bachelors—young ones in proportion. Address, Box 167. —BUTTERFLY."

SACK. I cut that out of the *Herald*, on Tuesday morning, answered it, and received in return the most delicate little note imaginable, on tinted paper, and in a disguised hand. The note enclosed this *carte de visite*. What do you think of it, Jack? (*Gives him picture.*)

BEN. Why, it's the full-faced view of the back of a lady's head.

SACK. A magnificent head of hair, isn't it, Jack? There's a head of back hair! How I long to see what's on the other side of that head of hair. I answered the note, asking the lady to meet me at this spot, at exactly nine o'clock this evening. I was to have a white rosebud, tied with a blue ribbon; she's to have a red, white and blue rosette on her shoulder—(*Music*)—in the place of a brooch—ha, ha, ha! Of course I haven't the remotest idea whether she will keep the engagement, but if—— (*Going up* R., *arm-in-arm.*)

BEN. If she does keep it, you'll have four women, instead of three, on your hands.

SACK. My dear Jack, there are at least 400,000 women

in New York, Brooklyn, Jersey City. I think four a very
reasonable number indeed.

BEN. But it isn't regular, my dear Bob ; it isn't regular.
                    [*They stroll out* R. 3. E.
  Enter EFFIE, *reading a piece of paper*, L. 1. E.

EFFIE. " X. Y. Z., or any other man. Which of you
wishes to correspond with an angel"—(*takes note from her
bosom*) " Caterpillar." I wonder what sort of a looking ge-
nius Caterpillar is? (*Reading.*) " My darling Butterfly !"
I didn't intend to answer any of them when I wrote the ad-
vertisement, but " Caterpillar" was so comical. " My darling Butterfly, I have fallen in love with your photograph.
There is a certain melancholy air about it. It is the most
expressive chignon I have ever seen." That's splendid ! If
I don't like "Caterpillar," I'll scamper back to pa, in the
West Room, like a deer. I'll stand demurely at his side, and
I'll defy any young man to so much as wink at me, when
my father gets his eye on him. (*Reading.*) " I enclose my
own picture. The face, as you will see, appeals strongly to
the imagination." (*Looking at picture.*) That's a splendid
portrait—of a gentleman's hat ! I am so anxious to find
out what kind of a moustache there is behind that hat.
                    [*Music* F. F. *People exit* R. *and* L
Enter SACKETT, R. 3. E. *He looks at ladies.* EFFIE *goes
and looks at gentlemen. Each dodging when discovered,
and staring at pictures.*

SACK. It's time for the red, white, and blue rosette to be
here.
Enter LIVINGSTON *and* OGDEN, *crossing* R. *and* L. SACKETT
                    looks closely at them.

SACK. Beg pardon, ladies. (*Aside.*) Nice girls, but no
rosettes.   [*Exit* E. S. L.

EFFIE. If the white rosebud doesn't come at all ! I'll be
so provoked.   [EFFIE *and* SACK. *meet* C., *they start.*

SACK. (L. C.). Effie !

EFFIE (R. C.). Robert !

SACK. She here ! the deuce ! If the red, white, and blue
rosette should appear at this moment !

EFFIE. He here ! and at such a time ! How provoking !
If the white rosebud should come along now !

SACK. (*embarrassed*). Ah, Effie !

EFFIE. Robert ! You almost took my breath away.
          [*They face each other, and recognize the signals they
                    wear.*

SACK. The red, white, and blue rosette !—

EFFIE. The white rose-bud ! Robert, then, is " Caterpillar !"

SACK. Effie is "Butterfly!" *(Looks at picture.)* Ah! Fool that I was! That back-hair!

EFFIE *(taking picture from her bosom).* Ah! That hat! the very same. So, sir, I have found you out. This is the way you remember your promises to me!

SACK. My memory seems to be quite as good as yours, Miss Remington.

EFFIE. Oh, Robert!

SACK. Ah! Effie!

EFFIE. Let's—let's both of us forgive each other?

SACK. My darling!   [*She takes his arm coquettishly.*

EFFIE. I—I—was only on a lark, you know, Robert.

SACK. And I was only trying to kill a little time by an innocent frolic. Besides *(holding out picture)* was it possible for me to look at that picture, and not recognize my Effie?

EFFIE. Ah!

SACK. That back-hair, which has so often rested on my shoulder;—every braid, every curl—every curl—each individual hair. I knew it was my Effie's back-hair.

Enter OLD REMINGTON, R. 3. E. *He pauses; puts on his spectacles; looks at them.*

EFFIE. And that hat, Robert,—*(holds up card)*—beneath whose shadow you and I have passed so many delightful moments. I was certain it was my Robert's hat, the crown, the brim, the band—everything told me it was my Robert's hat.

SACK. *and* EFFIE. A—h!
         [*He takes her two hands in his, warmly.*

OLD REM. *(loudly).* Ahem!   [EFFIE *goes up* C.

SACK. *(crossing to* REM. *confused).* May I trouble you for a light, sir?

OLD REM. I'm not smoking, sir.

SACK. Oh! Excuse me, sir.

OLD REM. You're not smoking, either, sir. This is no place to smoke in.

SACK. Eh? Oh—oh! so it isn't. I—I—I—beg pardon. Excuse me—but I—I—in fact—I am a little absent-minded now and then.

OLD REM. I see you are. Where there seems to be so much fire—egad, there ought to be *some* smoke. *(Crosses, and takes* EFFIE'S *arm.)* Come, daughter. *(Going* L. 1. R.; *turns to* SACK., *who is following.)* There is not room for three in the way which *we* are going, sir.

     Exeunt L. 1. E.   EFFIE *looking back, and kissing her hand to* ROBERT.   SACK. *looks off,* R. 3. E.

SACK. If there weren't any fathers in the world, there

wouldn't be any daughters, I suppose ; but, in my opinion, of all necessary evils, nature has inflicted mankind with a superfluity of fathers. 　　　　*[Stands, looking off* L.

Enter VIRGINIA *and* WETHERTREE, R. 1. E., *arm-in-arm.*

VIRG. (*sees* SACKETT). Ah ! Robert, my dear Robert !
　　　　　　　　　　　　　　　　[Crosses to him.

SACK. (*turning round*). Ah ! my darling Virginia ! I was thinking of you at this moment.

VIRG. Hush ! I forgot. Beg pardon, Mr. Wethertree— (*introducing*)—a friend of mine.　　　　　*[They bow.*

WETH. (R). Oh ! m—, m—, a friend of hers !

VIRG. (*aside*). We'll see each other to-morrow, Robert ?

SACK. (L). Certainly, my dear. I'll not think of another being until I meet you again.

VIRG. This way, Mr. Wethertree.
　　　　　　　[Takes his arm, and exeunt L. 3. E.

SACK. (*looking after her*). Virginia is so impulsive, so girlish, so gentle—every time I meet Virginia, I'm more and more in love with her.　　　　*[Still looking after her.*

Enter MRS. ALSTON *and* SIR MORTIMER, L. 1. C., *arm in-arm.*

MRS. A. We'll now try the West Room, Sir Mortimer. (*Crossing* R., *turns and sees* SACKETT.) Oh, Robert ! Mr. Sackett !　　　　　*[*SIR MORT. *goes up* R. *and down* L.

SACK. (*down* L.). My dear Mrs. Alston ! my dear Olivia ; my heart was full of your image at this very moment.

MRS. A. (*aside to him*). You did not meet me, yesterday, as usual, Robert.

SACK. A business engagement, my dear.

MRS. A. I will forgive you this time ; but you'll certainly call to-morrow afternoon ?

SACK. Most adorable of women, certainly I'll dream of nothing else till then.

MRS. A. (*sees* SIR MORT.). I beg pardon, Sir Mortimer. (*Crosses* L.) You'll excuse the interruption. We were going to the West Room, I believe.
　　　　　[Exeunt R. 1. E.　SACK. *looking after her.*

SACK. The widow's a charming woman—if she WAS an accident. I think I'm in love with her, after all ; in fact, the more I see of her——

Enter BENEDICT. R. *Arch.*

BEN. I say, Bob, have you got through ?

SACK. (*taking him* L. 3. E.). Ah ! Benedict, you're just in time—do you see her, Benedict ? Do you see Virginia ?

BEN. Yes ; that is, I see her back-hair, Bob.

SACK. "Her back-hair-bob"—nonsense. This way, Bene·

dict. -(*takes him* R. 1. E.)—the widow—[*music* P.]—do you
see her, Benedict—do you see her?

BEN. Yes ; I see her back-hair, Bob !

SACK. (*pulling him* L. 1. E.). And there, Benedict—(*enter guests as before*)—My darling Effie ; do you see her, Jack ?
—Do you see her?

BEN. Egad ! I'm not likely to see anything but back-hair,
Bob !

Enter GUESTS. *The* ARTIST *comes in* R. 1. E. LIVINGSTON
and OGDEN, R. *and* S.

SACK. (*turns each way*). Ah, Effie!--Virginia!—Olivia!
Benedict—Benedict—you have never loved as I love !

BEN. Heaven be praised, I never have !

[SACKETT *stumbles over a dress, and he falls through the
picture of " Cyrus the Great." General commotion ;
the* ARTIST *strikes an attitude* R. SACKETT *scrambles
to his feet, with his head through the canvas, and the
frame resting on his shoulders.*

CURTAIN.

END OF ACT FIRST.

ACT II.

SCENE.—*The Congress Springs at Saratoga ; interior of the
building, with roof and black and white marble pavement ;
the rising ground, walks, trees, &c., of the park in the back
ground. The sunken spring with its railing up* C.

*Discovered, the spring ; boy passing up water with long pole
and rack ; ladies and gentlemen passing* R. *and* L., *in the
park back, and drinking at the spring.* MUFFINS *leaning
against a pillar and knitting, over the rail of the spring ;
two children playing together back During* MUFFINS' *first
long speech, the different people, whom she describes, pass in,
drink. and pass out, with appropriate motions in dumbshow,
wry faces, &c.*

MUFFINS. Another glass of water for the ould lady ; I've
seen that same woman dhrink half a dozen glasses already this
blessed day, and she'll dhrink a dozen more before night—
she's been told it's the fashionable thing. There's the ould
coon wid de rheumatism again—along wid his wife—she's a
sharp one, she is—she makes him kape on dhrinking in
shpite of himself. She is anxious for a second husband, and
she thinks the rheumatism alone can't be depinded upon.
Och ! and there comes the man that always dhrinks whiskey
at night and Congress wather in the day-time. Divil a moment's pace does his poor stomach get day or night. One of

these days his stomach will go on a shtrike for eight hours'
work. And there comes the gintleman that's been in the
last stages of consumption for the last thirty-five years—the
ould darkey barber tould me all about it, and there's the
ould maid that went into a decline about the same time.
Sure it's a pity they didn't git married. It might have cured
them both, they've stood the wather all this time ; perhaps
they could 'a taken aitchither widout making a wry face at
the dose. Ah, bless her darling little heart! Here comes
the young lady that's thrying her best to learn how to drink
Congress wather, and look pritty at the same time—and the
young gintleman that's wid her, he's learning to endure disagreeable things widout swearing in the presence of ladies.
Sure they both have to retire together behind the curtains
in the bow window at the hotel before they can get the taste
of the water out of their mouths. I saw 'em there last night
fading aitchither wid swate mates. Och! and here she is
again—the big woman wid a little husband ; she's mighty
particular about his health—shure she—well may be too—
she'll niver git another if she loses him, and he's handy to
have in the house. She's awfully afraid he'll die—and he's
afraid he won't. There's wan thing I can't get through my
head, all the payple kape drinking this Saratogy water as if
there was a Chicago conflagration inside of 'em, and yit they
kape making faces all the time, as if they'd rather be swal-
lowing Kerasene oil ; bedad, I can't put this and that togither—ony more than I can the two sides of Misthress Gaylover's corsets. But Congress wather is the fashion, I suppose, and shure payple of fashion swallow worse things than
that every day ; faith, they swallow each other's compliments
widout making wry faces at all (*Leads children up stage*).

Enter REMINGTON, R. E.

REM. Boy, a glass of that damned water.
                                   [*Boy hands up water.*
        Enter VANDERPOOL, L. and E.
VAN. Boy! a glass of that damned water.
                [*Gets water ; they drink on opposite side.*
REM. Ah! Vanderpool!
VAN. Eh? oh! Remington.
REM. Enjoying your daily beverage, I suppose.
VAN. Eh? (*listening, his hand to his ears*).
REM. (*louder*). Your daily beverage.
VAN. Bev-beverage?   Y-e-s. My doctor prescribed it.
I asked him to make it castor-oil, but he wouldn't relent.
REM. I've been practising—on petroleum.
VAN. Petroleum! yes ; they say they do use petroleum

now—instead of old shoes. I'm getting along, however.
I've been taking a few easy lessons in paragoric (*sips*). Delicious, isn't it? (*wry face*).

REM. (*sipping, with a wry face*). Delightful.

VAN. Nectar.

REM. (*coming down* R., *wiping his forehead*). They call this
travelling for pleasure—thermometer at ninety-eight in——

VAN. Eh! what say?

REM. I say the thermometer is ninety-eight in——

VAN. Yes—in a refrigerator. Mrs. Vanderpool, and **my**
daughter, Virginia, call this travelling for pleasure.

REM. So does my daughter, Effie, heigh-hi—unfortunately,
I have no wife to share the pleasure with me.

VAN. Eh! what did you say was unfortunate?

REM. I say I have no wife to——

VAN. Oh! m – m—y-e-s—that's a matter of opinion.

REM. I regard it as very unfortunate, indeed.

VAN. M-m—y-e-s—some folks do.

REM. (*loudly in his ear*). I feel the want of a mother's care
for my daughter Effie.

VAN. Mother's care, daughter? Don't trouble yourself
about that, old fellow—your girl will be married soon enough
without a mother's care; my daughter, Virginia, has a
mother's care—too much—by half.

REM. But a mother can watch over——

VAN. Watch? yes—Mrs. Vanderpool is always on the
watch, Mrs. Vanderpool watches a young gentleman as a cat
watches a mouse.

REM. As to my daughter Effie—I can't do anything with
the girl She is even now off to the races—alone—with two
gentlemen.

VAN. Race—yes! it's a race between the women in Saratoga who'll get to the devil first—up to one o'clock in the
morning at a hop—breakfast at eleven.

REM. Then come the horse races at the park.

VAN. Dressing.

REM. (*in his ear*). Dinner.

VAN. More dressing.

REM. Another hop in the evening (*in his ear*).

VAN. And after that—the Lord knows what—I don't.
That is what Mrs. Vanderpool calls "travelling for pleasure."

REM. (*going* R. *with* VAN.). *Damn* travelling for pleasure.

VAN. Eh?

REM. I say—I—I don't—like travelling for pleasure.

VAN. Neither do I—*damn* travelling for pleasure!

> [*Exeunt together* R. E., *during above conversation
> people have passed and repassed in park, and also*

in the colonnade, getting water, MUFFINS *leaning over the railing ; the children playing at back.*

LITTLE GIRL (*looking up from her play*). Oh! Muffins—there's mamma, and papa—both together.

MUFFINS (*looking R.*). Their mother and their father both together. That's a very remarkable coincidence (*emphasis on third syl.*). I notice they're always togither when they're quarrelling—and visy versy—they're always quarrelling whin they're togither. They've parted agin. I thought they wouldn't bay long togither widout laving aitchither. Now she's coming this way wid Major Luddington Whist. Here comes your mamma, my little dears - mind you don't disturb her by spaking to her.

Enter MRS. GAYLOVER *on the arm of* MAJOR LUDDINGTON WHIST. *They pass slowly to* L.

MRS. GAY. Ha—ha—ha—what would my husband say if he should hear that, my dear Major?

THE MAJOR. What would he say? I don't know, upon my life. I could guess what he would *think*, however.

MRS. GAY. And what would he *think*, pray?

THE MAJOR. He would think that it was exactly what he himself had said—to some other gentleman's wife—within the last twenty-four hours.

MRS. GAY. Ha—ha—ha—I fear you are a very naughty man, indeed, Major Luddington Whist.

THE MAJOR. My dear madam—the word "naughty" in a woman's vocabulary—when app'ied to the opposite sex—is charity itself; it covers a multitude of sins.

LITTLE GIRL. Mamma! [*The two chilirn run to her.*

MRS. GAY. Oh! my children (*pushing them aside*). My dress—you will ruin it (*they turn aside crying and clinging to* MUFFINS). Muffins, don't allow the children to disturb me while I am dressing for dinner. Excuse the interruption, Major Whist (*takes his arm going* L., *turns*). And Muffins—I shall need a long nap after dinner—see that the children do not enter my room (*going, turns*). And Muffins, put the children to bed immediately after supper. I shall be dressing for the ball at the Clarendon. And I shall need your assistance ;--and Muffins, don't allow the children to disturb their father this afternoon—it makes him nervous—sorry to keep you so long, Major.

THE MAJOR. Don't mention it, madam—domestic matters *will* sometimes intrude even upon the sacred duties of society (*shows her out—exeunt* L. E.).

MUFFINS. What are you in this world for, anyway, the little cherubins? Ye ware niver sent for. Why didn't ye stay in Heaven where they apprayciate little children. It's lucky you've got some one to love, bless your little hearts, if it isn't anybody but Muffins. For all they say of their father and mither in Saratoga, they might as well bay in the orphan asylum. I was hired for a nurse—and I have to be father and mither, too, to these blessed infants—all for eighteen shillings a wake. [*Exit* B. *with children.*

Enter OGDEN B., *and* LIVINGSTON B. *and* L.

OGDEN. Livingston!

LIVINGSTON. Ogden!

OGDEN (*coming down*). Just back from the races? Weren't they splendid to-day?

LIV. I think they were horrid. I lost forty dollars.

OGDEN. Ha. ha! of course they were horrid—you didn't bet on the right horse, that was all.

Enter VIRGINIA, *followed by* LITTLEFIELD, L. E.

VIRGINIA. Oh! here you are. girls (*turning to* LITTLEFIELD). That will do, Frank, you may leave now. After dinner, you know, then you may make love to me again—I'm tired now.

[LITTLEFIELD *bows and exits* L., VIRGINIA *comes down.*

Girls—been to the races, of course—I got back ahead of you all, Major Luddington Whist was with me, you know—and he drives such splendid horses; we took the longest way around too. We passed everything on the road as if it were standing still. Jenny Hazleton and her lover took our dust before we had been out of the park three minutes. Then we came up to old Wethertree and Effie Remington, ha—ha—ha—then there *was* fun. Effie seized the ribbons herself—so did I—we couldn't trust the men at such a time as that, you know. It was neck and neck for a moment—one word from the Major—and the last Remington saw of us was the back of my head as we whirled round the corner, and came in on the same stretch—ha—ha—ha—the Major is a charming fellow—he puts a girl behind such splendid horses. Here comes Remington, under double convoy. She's been doing the spoony with Wethertree and Sir Mortimer alternately for the last two weeks.

OGDEN. They say she's engaged to Mr. Wethertree.

LIVINGSTON. Is it true?

VIRGINIA. He proposed to her last evening. She will probably accept him—for the season.

[*All laugh—going up* L., *get water.*

Enter EFFIE *with* SIR MORTIMER *and* WETHERTREE, B. E.

EFFIE (*significantly, as if dismissing him*). Good-afternoon, Sir Mortimer.

SIR MORT. Eh! Y—e—s. Very delightful afternoon.

WETH (*aside*). He! he! that is a pretty broad hint Sir Mortimer. He! he! he!

EFFIL (*in same manner*). Good afternoon, Mr. Wethertree!

WETH. Eh! yes! a particularly pleasant day.

EFFIE (*demurely, after looking at each*, C.). I have had sufficient for the present.

SIR MORT. Ah, yes; certainly (*moves* L.).

WETH. Exactly. Ahem! Certainly. Good morning, Miss Remington. (*Bows and exit* L. 1. E.)

SIR MORT. (*aside*). These American girls are the most unaccountable creatures. They pick a man up, and then they drop him: one never knows when he is going to be dropped, you know (*looks at* EFFIE, *who stands looking at him demurely*). Y—e—s. *Au revoir*, Miss Effie (*aside*); I am dropped. These American girls are the most unaccountable creatures. [*Exit* R. 1. E.

EFFIE. Ha! ha! ha! Congratulate me, girls! Ha! ha! Old Wethertree and Sir Mortimer Muttonlegg each wants me to be the wife of his bosom, respectively. Ha! ha! ha! Imagine me the wife of Old Wethertree's bosom.

ALL Ha! ha! ha! ha!

VIRGINIA (L. C.). And Frank Littlefield, the student, you know, asked me to be the wife of *his* bosom yesterday afternoon. So did Major Luddington. Whist!

EFFIE (R. C.) What's a poor girl to do? She can't be the wife of everybody's bosom.

VIRG. (L. C.). How much did you lose at the races, Effie?

EFFIE. Lose? I won thirty-five dollars. I bet on Hamburg.

VIRG. Why, Hamburg was the last horse in. How did you win thirty-five dollars, if you bet on the horse that was beaten?

EFFIE. Why, Old Wethertree *said* I won; and a young girl isn't expected to know anything about such things, you know. When the race was over, I pouted my lips, and looked injured, you know, and says I, "There—I've lost my bet!" "No, you haven't, my dear," said he; "you've won the bet." All I said was, "Oh!"

ALL THE GIRLS. Oh! (*long drawn out*).

EFFIE. And Wethertree passed over the stakes.

VIRG. Ha! ha! ha! the designing wretch!

EFFIE. To impose on a young girl's innocence in that way (*laugh*). But what'll we do with the money, girls? Oh! I have it. You know that old woman who sells apples and sugar-things by the spring? She told me yesterday that her eldest boy had broken his leg, and she's got to support the family and pay the doctor's bill besides. I'm going to give my money to her.

2

VIRG. (L C.). And I won sixty dollars. I'll give my sixty. That'll make ninety-five-dollars for the old woman.

EFFIE. That'll be jolly : she never had so much money in her life before !

OGDEN (R. E.). I must go and dress for dinner.

LIVINGSTON. So must I.

EFFIE. Oh! there's plenty of time for that. Come along, Vanderpool : let's take a turn in the park. They talk about a girl's needing two hours to dress for dinner—I can jump out of a walking-dress into a trail in exactly ten minutes by the clock. [*Exeunt* EFFIE *and* VIRGINIA, R. 1. E., OGDEN *and* LIVINGSTON, L. 1. E.

Enter BENEDICT, L. 1. E.

BEN. (*looking off* R.). Mrs. Olivia Alston and Olivia walking alone in the park with Colonel Tillinghart again. That is the third time I've seen them together within —— Well. what the deuce do I care if Mrs. Olivia Alston is walking in the park with another gentleman ? It's no affair of mine. What the deuce am I mop ng around and watching every movement as jealously as if—if Mrs. Olivia Alston chooses to—— Jack Benedict, you're a fool ! It is perfectly ridiculous; to fall in love with a woman ; to be jilted by her ; to see her marry another man ; and to fall in love with the same woman again. after she becomes a widow ! It is perfectly ridiculous ! I know it : and I can't help it ; it isn't the regular thing—I'll be the laughing-stock of all my friends (*looks at watch*). There! I've been letting my watch run down again. I've done that twice this week. Somehow I can t be regular in anything now.

Enter SACKETT, *in travelling-suit ; comes down* R. *of* BEN, *slapping him on the shoulder.*

SACKETT. Hallo! Jack !

BEN. What! Bob Sackett!

SACK (*rapidly*). Jack, you're the very man I want. I've been looking for you everywhere ! Don't ask any questions —there isn't time (*looks* R. *and* L.). Jack, I dare not remain within the city limits of Saratoga five minutes. I stand upon a powder-magazine (BENEDICT *starts*). Effie, Virginia, and the widow are all in Saratoga. I expect an explosion any moment.

BEN. All in Saratoga? Then why are you here ?

SACK. Fate, my dear Benedict !—Fate ! I am here to ask a favour of you, Jack. I discovered that my three dulcineas were all here, just in time, you know, *not* to come myself. So I wrote to Effie, Virginia, and the widow, that professional duties detained me in New York. Well—" professional duties " called me to Vermont, about three weeks ago ; hunting, fishing, dancing, and so on, among the Green Mountains—anywhere except Saratoga. A few days ago, as I was walking by a lake near the Mansfield Mountain House, in the moonlight, I saw a runaway horse dashing madly down the road. As it came nearer, I discovered a fair young creature.

BEN. (*starting*). Another woman !

SACK. Another woman ! no, sir—an angel ! I sprang into the middle of the road ; the horse stopped suddenly before me. and the fair young creature fell over the dashboard into my arms. On the impulse of the moment I pressed a dozen warm kisses on her lips. That is all I have to remember her by ; a beastly young brother came up in a moment. She thanked me in the politest possible language, and that is the last I've seen of her. I've not had a moment's peace since that night. Such an exquisite throat ; and a wealth of golden hair fell back upon her shoulders ! Unknown enchantress of my life—my fair incognita !—I—

BEN. But what has all this to do with your visit to Saratoga?

SACK. (R.). I hurried to the Mansfield House next morning. She had been there. but had left two hours before. The party, so far as I could learn, consisted of an elderly gentleman—her father, of course—the angel herself, and her brother. I traced them to Lake George ; from there they had started for Saratoga ; and here I am in search of the golden fleece——

BEN. (L.). Well, now you're here, you can share my private parlour—No. 73.

SACK. My dear Benedict, I couldn't think of it. I dare not remain in Saratoga five minutes. I don't propose to run into any more danger than is necessary. I intend to engage rooms at the Driftwood House, near the banks of the lake. And now my favour from you, Jack. I want you to stare at every woman in Saratoga ; look every old gentleman out of countenance——until you find my fair unknown. Remember. Jack, she has a profusion of golden tresses. an oval face, medium height, an elderly father, and a young brother. Search every hotel in Saratoga, hire the fastest horses you can get, and report to me, at least three times a day, at the Driftwood House. If you find her, Jack, I'll leave the rest to chance and Providence. I'll follow her to the ends of the earth. By-the-way. Jack, how do you get along among the Saratoga belles ? No fluttering about the heart, now and then, you old icicle—eh ?

BEN. (L.). Ahem ! Well, I say, Bob, you'll promise not to laugh at me ?

2—2

SACK. Oh! eh! Not—ha! ha! ha!—then there is—ha! ha! Oh, certainly! I'll promise not to laugh—ha! ha! ha! (*checks himself*).

BEN. (L.). Well, then—I—I—I *am* in love—with a widow, Bob.

SACK. A widow?—ha! ha! ha! ha!—(*checks himself*).

BEN. Bob, I—I—I—am in love with the same woman I was in love with before she was married.

SACK. The—ha! ha! ha! ha! ha!—I know I promised not to laugh, Jack; but—ha! ha! ha!—the *same* woman that you were —ha! ha! ha! Does being a widow improve her any, Jack? Ha! ha! ha!—I say, Jack, you waited for the second table, didn't you?—ha! ha! ha! You took her affections warmed over. By-the-way, Jack, what is the widow's name?—ha! ha! ha!

BEN. Her name—Mrs. O'ivia Alston! (SACK. *stops laughing, draws a long face, and staggers*). Eh! what's the matter, Bob?

SACK. Nothing; only a little stitch in the side. (*Aside*) It's *my* widow!

BEN. (*looking* R.). There she is now, Ben, coming this way, with a gentleman. She'll be here in two minutes. I'll introduce you.

SACK. No, thank you, Jack. I have a very particular engagement elsewhere at this particular moment. I wish you joy, old boy: and, by-the-way, Jack, kiss the widow now and then on *my* account—ha! ha! ha!—and you'll not forget the Driftwood House, Benedict?

BEN. Certainly not. I am to stare at every woman in Saratoga.

SACK. A flood of go'den tresses—

BEN. (R.). Report three times a day—

SACK. (L.). The fastest horses you can get.

BEN. Ha! ha! ha!   [*Exit* R.

SACK. Ha! ha! ha!—*his* widow—*my* widow!   [*Exit* L.

Enter MR. *and* MRS. VANDERPOOL, R. U. E.

MRS. VAN. (L.). Mr. Vanderpool, you're a brute!

VAN. (*putting hand to his ear*). What say?

MRS. VAN. (*in his ear*). You are a brute!

VAN. Y-e-s—very likely, my dear; you told me that thirty years ago, my love.

MRS. VAN. If I had told it to you every day in the year, for thirty years, I should only have been doing my duty.

VAN. (R.). Well, my dear, I don't think there are many days in the last thirty years that need rest very heavily on your conscience. If I had my way about it, Mrs. Vanderpoor, Virginia should not remain another day in Saratoga.

Look at the girl to-day, madam; she has come home from the races with her head full of chestnut fillies, and three-year-old geldings, and little bay mares, and quarter poles, and pedigrees. If I had my way about it, madam, Virginia shouldn't remain at Saratoga another hour.

MRS. VAN. (L.). But you haven't your way about it. Mr. Vanderpool! Virginia shall remain in Saratoga until the 15th of September. You insist on burying the girl in some quiet resort by the seaside for the summer;—now, I insist on giving her all the advantages of fashionable society. Virginia is of a marriageable age, Mr. Vanderpool, and *I* am a mother.

VAN. You certainly are, my dear.

MRS. VAN. You are a father!

VAN. I certainly am—that is, I presume I am, Mrs. Van-derpool.

MRS. VAN. We each of us owe a duty to Virginia. My duty is that of a careful mother. Young gentlemen of the very best families come to Saratoga. Would you have me neglect my duty, Mr. Vanderpool?

VAN. (R.). But the girl has already been engaged to three gentlemen to my positive knowledge. It isn't a mother's duty to provide more than one husband for her female off-spring, is it?

MRS. VAN. Mr. Vanderpool, I was engaged to *four* gentle-men before I married you.

VAN. Y-e-s—I remember. I never forgave that last fellow for dropping off so suddenly just before I —

MRS. VAN. Vanderpool!

VAN. Eh?

Enter HON. WM. CARTER *and* LUCY, L. 1. E.

CARTER. This way, my dear—boy, a glass of water. Shall I hold your shawl, my dear?

LUCY. Thank you, my love (*gives him shawl, and takes water*). Ah—oh! isn't it horrid, though?

VAN. (R. C.). Why, surely—certainly, it is my old friend —William Carter!

CARTER (L. C.). Eh! Why, my dear Vanderpool!—de-lighted to meet you at Saratoga—it must be five years, at least, since we have seen each other—Mrs. Vanderpool, too? This is an unexpected pleasure. Mrs. Carter—my wife—Mrs. Vanderpool—(MRS. VAN. *and* LUCY *bow*)—Mrs. Carter, this is one of my very best old friends—Mr. Vanderpool (*passing her over to* VAN.).

VAN. (R. C.). Why, upon my word, that's very odd. I knew you had a son, old fellow, but I certainly never saw your daughter before.

CARTER (L. C. R., *aside*). That's pleasant, by Jove! that's the tenth time my wife has been taken for my daughter since we've been on our wedding tour.

VAN. I'm delighted to see you, my little darling—he! he! he! (*pats her under the chin*). I've known your father ever since he was a boy, my dear—we were schoolmates together —he! he! he!—I shall be your *uncle*, you know—he! he! he! You must call me " Uncle," for the sake of Auld Lang Syne (*kisses her*).

MRS. VAN. (R.). Vanderpool!

VAN. Eh? (*kisses* LUCY *again*).

CARTER (*aside*). Vanderpool chucks my wife under the chin and kisses her for the sake of Auld Lang Syne. Damn Auld Lang Syne!

VAN. I knew your mother very well, my dear.

CARTER. Ahem!

VAN. Your mother was a lovely woman, my dear: one of the most angelic women I ever met.

CARTER (L., *aside*). Oh, Lord! my first wife!

VAN. But she must have died before you can remember. Let me see—seventeen years ago—of course you can't remember it.

CARTER (*aside*). Confound *his* memory, say I!

MRS. VAN. Mr. Vanderpool, this lady is the *wife* of Mr. Carter (*in his ear*, R.).

VAN. Eh! what?

MRS. VAN. (*in his ear*). This lady is not his daughter—— *wife!*

VAN. Not his daughter——wife! Oh, she's your son's wife! Well, I thought it was curious; but it's all in the family, isn't it, my little dear?—he! he! he! (*chucks her chin, and kisses her*).

CARTER. Damn it, Vanderpool, the lady is *my* wife! (*in his ear*).

VAN. Eh!

CARTER (*in his ear*). Mrs. Carter—is *my* wife!

VAN. (R. C.). Your—she is your wife—ha—ha—ha—(*laughs very heartily some seconds*). I say, my dear—suppose—ha— ha—ha—you—ha—ha—were—ha—ha—were — ha — ha — such a tender young thing as that! (*pointing with his thumb to* LUCY, *and still laughing*).

MRS. V. (*with dignity*). Mr. Vanderpool—I was *once* such a tender young thing as that.

VAN. Yes—but then—I was a tender young thing too—I say, Carter, you old rogue, why didn't you keep inside your own generation—ha—ha—ha—(*punching his ribs*). By-the-way, old boy, you must forgive me for kissing your wife—

you may take your revenge if you like—by kissing Mrs.
Vanderpool—ha—ha!   [*They go up* R. C.
Enter EFFIE *and* VIRGINIA, R.

EFFIE *and* VIRG. Lucy Martindale!

LUCY. Effie Remington and Virginia Vanderpool! (*kisses
them*). Not Lucy Martindale now, girls. I'm married now,
you know.

EFFIE. Oh! yes, we heard you were going to get married.

VIRG. I say, Carter, is that your husband?

LUCY. Yes! isn't he a nice old gentleman?

EFFIE. How do you like the old man, Carter?

VAN. By-the-way, Carter, old boy—you and—and—ha—
ha—and your—wife—have arrived just in the nick of time.
We've arranged for a picnic this afternoon out at the lake :—
Mrs. Vanderpool—Remington—the girls, Benedict, Mrs.
Alston, and the rest of us--half-past three—you'll join us,
of course.

CARTER. Oh--certainly ;—Mrs. Carter and I will join the
party with pleasure—eh, my love?

LUCY. (*nodding*). Certainly, my darling.

VAN. He—he—" Mrs. Carter"—wife !—he—he—" my
love "—" darling " –he—he—o-h !—Carter—ha ha - ha—
(*punching him in the ribs*).
Enter FRED. CARTER. L. *He is dressed in the height of fashion,
glasses, cane, &c.*

FRED. Hallo! governor—mother dear, I thought you had
gone to your room at the hotel.

VAN. (R. C. *to Carter*). Certainly. I recognize him at once.

MRS. V. This is your son, Frederic?

VAN. Such a striking resemb'ance to his mother, the first
Mrs. Carter—your angelic predecessor, my dear.

LUCY (*introducing Fred.*). My son, Frederic Augustus
Carter, Miss Vanderpool (*they bow*). My son, Miss Remington (*they bow*).

EFFIE (*aside to* VIRG.). I say, Vanderpool, isn't Carter
putting on airs?

VIRG. Introducing that great fellow as her son !

EFFIE. She's only been married three weeks. I'll be his
grandmother.

FRED. (*crossing to* L. C.). Delighted to meet you, ladies;
in fact I'm delighted to get to Saratoga, where they have
billiards and cards, and ladies, and fairs, and races, and everything else to make a gentleman comfortable. Father, mother,
and I have been on our wedding tour.

CARTER (L.). Have we?

VAN. (R. C.). Oh, yes, I say, Carter, you haven't told us
about your wedding tour yet, of course.

MRS. VAN. (R.). Yes, you must tell us all about your wedding tour.

FRED. (L. C.). Certainly. We had a delightful wedding tour; we've been to the Green Mountains, White Mountains, and Lake George—balls, moonlight walks, music.

CARTER (*turning him away by the ear*). I'd like to know who's wedding tour this is.

FRED. (*recovering his position*). And such an adventure as mother had when we were at the Mansfield Mountain House in Vermont.

LUCY (L. C.). Oh. yes! it was so funny. Frederic and I were riding alone, near the lake, in the moonlight, one evening. Mr. Carter wasn't very well that evening.

CARTER. Yes, a slight cold, which—ah! had settled in my limbs.

VAN. Eh! Oh yes; that isn't what I call it.

CARTER. Never mind what you call it, sir. Mrs. Carter was riding alone with Frederic.

LUCY. Yes; and the horse suddenly took fright as we reached a dangerous part of the road. Frederic was thrown out at the first bound.

FRED. Yes—ha--ha—ha—I landed plump in a puddle of water. (*All laugh.*)

LUCY. And I was left alone in the carriage. Of course I was terribly frightened—I don't know what might have become of me, but just as I was approaching a dangerous turn in the road—a man——

VIRG. (R. C.). A man?

EFFIE (C.). A man? It begins to get interesting.

LUCY. A man sprang into the centre of the road. The horse stopped as suddenly as it had started—and I——

CARTER. Mrs. Carter fell over the dashboard.

LUCY. Into the arms of the—arms of—

EFFIE. Of the man.

CARTER. Exactly. Mrs. Carter fell over the dashboard into the arms—of the man.

VAN. Mr. Carter should be eternally grateful to—the man.

CARTER. So I am. I shall never forgive—I mean I shall never forget that—man.

LUCY. Frederic came up in a moment, we thanked the stranger and—and that was the last we saw of him. He was a *young* man.

VIRG. Oh! he was a young man.

CARTER (L.). Some young snipe or another.

LUCY. Yes; he was some young snipe or another. He was of about medium height, and he—he had a moustache—I am certain he had a moustache.

VIRG. That kind of "snipe" always does have a moustache.

EFFIE. And a woman can nearly always tell it just as well in the dark as she can in the daytime.

LUCY. Oh! but it was moonlight, you know.

CARTER. Certainly. It was moonlight.

VAN. Yes, moonshine. [*The party separate and all move up*

Enter MRS. ALSTON *and* BENEDICT, R. E.

MRS. A. How very romantic, Mr. Benedict.

BEN. My friend is perfectly enthusiastic about the lady. A flood of golden tresses, you know.

MRS. A. Ha—ha—ha—and such an exquisite throat (*sees others*). Ah! Virginia. Effie, Mrs. Vanderpool, we have all a mission to perform (*all come forward*) for Cupid,* a friend of Mr. Benedict—he refuses to tell me his name—for that he says is confidential—is hovering around Saratoga, in search of an unknown fairy, whose shadow he is determined to follow to the ends of the world.

EFFIE (C.). Oh! a romance.

LUCY (L. C.). A romance!

MRS. VAN. (R.). By-the-way, Mrs. Alston, Mrs. Carter—the Hon. William Carter, her husband, Mr. Frederic Augustus Carter (*they bow*), Mr. Benedict (*he bows*).

BEN. (L. C.). Yes—ha—ha—ha—my friend has commissioned me to stare at every lady in Saratoga. Now that's no light task for a modest gentleman like myself, and I shall ask all you ladies to assist me.

MRS. VAN. Certainly—we will be delighted to assist you.

BEN. I'm to discover a very beautiful young creature with a flood of golden hair, falling back upon her shoulders, an oval face, and medium height. She is accompanied by her father, an elderly gentleman, and a young brother. My friend me the young lady under very peculiar circumstances, on a lonely road near the Mansfield Mountain House, in Vermont.

CARTER (L.) (*interested*). Where did you say he met the lady, sir?

BEN. Upon a lonely road near the Mansfield Mountain House, in Vermont. The lady was in a carriage alone—her horse was dashing madly down the road (*sensation*).

LUCY (L. C.). Ahem! Mr. Benedict.

BEN. Eh!

OMNES (*in succession*). Go on, sir—go on, Mr. Benedict—go on, &c., &c.

\   * NOTE.—Position as they come forward.

	Mrs. Alston, Effie.
Virginia.	Benedict.
Mrs. Vanderpool.	Lucy.
Vanderpool.	Carter.
	Frederic.

2—3

BEN. Certainly. I *was* going on, and so was the horse, by-the-way. The animal dashed madly down the road, bearing its lovely freight to destruction.

MRS. A. (C.). But Mr. Benedict's friend saw the danger, and sprang into the road.

BEN. The horse stopped suddenly before him—and the fair young creature——

CARTER. Fell over the dashboard into the arms of **your** friend.

BEN. Exactly—and I leave it to you, sir, if, under similar circumstances, you wouldn't have fallen in love with the girl yourself.

CARTER. Hang it, sir, you n, edn't leave anything to me, sir.

OMNES (*in succession*). Go on—go on, Mr. Benedict—go on—

BEN. Ha—ha—ha.—He is most desperately in love with her—raves about her exquisitely moulded throat—her ruby lips—her ——

LUCY. Ah! Mr. Benedict.

OMNES (*in succession*). Go on, sir—go on, Mr. Benedict—go on.

BEN. I *am* going on. He calls her the unknown enchantress of his soul—an angel incognita—ha—ha—swears he will follow her to the ends of the earth.

CARTER. Oh, he will—will he?

LUCY. Oh! Mr. Benedict—sir——

BEN. Eh!

OMNES (*in succession*). Go on—go on, Mr. Benedict—go on.

BEN. Ha—ha—poor fellow, he has nothing to remember her by, not even her name, except the memory of a dozen warm kisses——

LUCY. Ah! (*screams*).

OMNES (*in concert. with great vigour*). Go on—go on, Mr. Benedict—go on.

BEN. Which he *pressed upon her lips.*

LUCY. A-h!

VIRGINIA and EFFIE. Ha—ha—ha—ha!

EFFIE. She was certain he had a moustache.

BEN. Why, the lady is not well (LUCY *falls into his arms*).

EFFIE. Let's every one of us faint!

[*General movement.* CARTER *up* R. *and down* C., *where* EFFIE *and* VIRGINIA *fall into his arms. Meantime* MRS. ALSTON *falls into* VANDERPOOL'S *arms. He sees* MRS. VANDERPOOL *staggering.* BENEDICT *tosses* MRS. CARTER *to* FRED. VANDERPOOL *tosses* MRS. ALSTON *to*

BENEDICT, *and* MRS. VANDERPOOL *falls heavily into* VANDERPOOL'S *arms.   Picture.*

VERY QUICK CURTAIN.

ACT III.

SCENE.—*Woodland.   Picnic ground on the shore of Saratoga Lake.   Foliage profuse.*

Picnic party discovered.   Remnant of repast.   A cloth laid out, C., *with chicken, bread-plates, knives and forks, some cold meat, wine cooled with champagne.* VANDERPOOL *opening bottle of champagne,* L. C.   GYP *dodging cork.* WETH. *and* SIR MORT., R., *offering wine to* EFFIE, *who is seated on stump* R. *up stage.*   MRS. VAN. *seated on a rock,* L. 3. E. MRS. CARTER. R. *of* C.; CARTER *at back walking about.*   VIRGINIA *and* LITTLEFIELD *seated on bank,* L. 1. E. OGDEN *and* LIVINGSTON *seated,* R. 1. E., *on bank.*

Music at rise.—A ballad sung by one of the ladies, with chorus by all.

VAN. (*pouring wine*). Ha, ha, ha.   This is the merriest day I've had in many a year.   Mrs. Vanderpool, allow me—can I trouble you for another glass, Lucy?   Thank you, my dear.   Shall I fill it for you?

LUCY (R. C.).   No, thank you, Mr. Vanderpool.

VAN. "Uncle" Vanderpool, my dear.

LUCY. Uncle Vanderpool, I'll not take any more wine, thank you, "uncle."   I prefer water.

VAN. That's right, my dear, water was made before wine, and is better for you young folk.   But we old coons need a little stimulant now and then, don't we, Carter?   Don't we, Mrs. Vanderpool?

MRS. VAN. Mr. Vanderpool, I am not an "old coon."

VAN. I'll not insist upon the "coon," my dear.

CARTER. Mrs. Carter, it is getting late, we had better return to the carriages.

Enter BEN *and* MRS. ALSTON R. 1. E., *come forward* C.

BEN (*looking at watch*). Exactly half-past five, we agreed to be home at half-past six.   We must——

MRS. ALSTON. We haven't to meet a railroad train—there is plenty of time, we will continue our stroll, Mr. Benedict (*going* L.)

BEN. But, my dear, we agreed to return before half-past six—and—and—

MRS. ALSTON. And we shall do nothing of the kind.   I am going down the path in this direction—there is a very pretty lane.   Don t mind us, Mrs. Vanderpool.   Mr. Benedict and I have a carriage of our own, you know.

BEN. But my dear Olivia—we agreed to—we promised——
MRS. ALSTON. I am going in this direction.   [*Exit L.*
BEN. I—ahem (*wavers*)—somehow or other I never *can*
keep an appointment now. I can't be regular in anything.
                                                    [*Exit after her.*
LUCY (*suddenly starting*). Oh !
VAN. Eh! (*comes to her*).
CARTER. What is it, my darling ?
LUCY. I thought I heard a gun.
VAN. A gun ?
LUCY. I was always afraid of guns (*a distant gun heard*).
There—yes—I was certain of it. There is somebody hunt-
ing in these woods.
CARTER. Nonsense, my love, they are not hunting for such
little tame ducks as you.
LUCY (*pouting*). I am not a little tame duck, I nearly
fainted once when I heard a gun, anyway.
VAN. There, there my little pet—Uncle Vanderpool won't
let anybody hurt it, to be sure. (*Pats her under the chin
and kisses her*. MRS. VAN. *checks him*. CARTER *disgusted*).
EFFIE (*suddenly*). I want some wine (*holds glass*). (SIR
MORT. *and* WETH. *both run, one with sherry the other with
claret, which they get from* GYP).
WETH. Claret, Miss Effie ?   }
SIR MORT. Sherry, Miss Remington ?   } *together.*
EFFIE. Thank you, gentlemen, but I never take wine
fixed ; I prefer it " straight " (*both gentlemen come down
owning at each other*). Well, aren't you going to give me any
wine at all ? (*They hasten back, she holds out two glasses,* SIR
MORT. *pours in* L. *and* WETH. R.) That's what I call
" neutrality."
            [LUCY *directs* GYP *to gather up the things; he and*
                VAN. *commence packing them in large basket.*
VIRG. (L.). You have read so many books, Mr. Littlefield.
LITTLEFIELD. I have read more from your eyes, Miss Virginia, than from all the books I ever owned. You have
opened a volume to me in which I find a new philosophy.
VAN. Come, Virginia, they are gathering up the things to
return.
VIRG. (R.) (*rising*). Mr. Littlefield and I will return before
the carriages are ready ; papa, we will only stroll down into
the dell and back.
LITTLEFIELD. Besides, Miss Virginia and I came in a carriage of our own, you know.   [*Exeunt arm in arm* R. 1. E.
VAN. (*aside*). Virginia and Mr. Littlefield have been sitting under that tree by themselves all the afternoon. That

looks like business.   I only hope the little gipsy isn't flirting
with him.

EFFIE. There, Sir Mortimer, you carry that (*giving him
shawl*). Wethertree, you carry this (*gives him goblets and nap-
kins*).

VAN. Here Gyp, take that basket.   I'll carry this (*takes
bucket with wine*).   Mrs. Vanderpool, we will let the young
folks bring each other.

[*Exit* GYP, MR. *and* MRS. VAN., MR. CARTER *and*
LUCY, L. 3. *and* 2. E.

EFFIE (*seeing table-cloth*). Oh!   Mr. Wethertree, there's
the table-cloth (*throws it over him*).   Sir Mortimer, you
carry that (*gives him basket*), Mr. Wethertree, there's the
water pitcher—Sir Mortimer, there's a fork—that's enough
—now come along.

[*Exit with* WETH. *and* SIR MORT. ; *as she is going out
she first takes the a· m of one, then stops suddenly and
takes the arm of the othe· also.*
Re-enter LUCY, L. 3 E.

LUCY. I think they've got everything—it won't hurt to
look, however (*looks about on grass, &c.*)   Let me see, the
silver cream pitcher—I wonder if that was put in either of
the baskets—I came near forgetting all about it (*looks* R. *and*
L.) (*Gun fired* R. 2. E.)

LUCY (*screams*). Oh !
Enter SACKETT *backwards, a short gun in his hands in full
hunting gear looking off* R.

SACKETT. Egad, she's fluttering—a second shot will bring
her down.   (*Fires gun again.*)

LUCY (*screams*). Oh ! (*staggering;* SACKETT *turns in time
to catch her with* LUCY *in his arms*).

SACKETT. Another duck, by Jove !   No—it's quite a
different bird.   It's a regular wood nymph !   (*He sits up
stump* C., LUCY *in his arms*).   Oh, can I believe my eyes,
certainly I can.   The fairy of my dreams.   The unknown
angel who fell into my arms from heaven itself·-or rather
from a one-horse buggy, near the Mansfield Mountain House,
in Vermont.   Those lips, how well I remember them.   Delicious burden (*kisses her*).   I once took a course of medical
lectures, and I remember among other instructions, that in
case a lady fainted, it was always best to move her as little
as possible.   I shall allow her to remain in the place in which
she originally fell.

MRS. VAN. (*without* L.).   Lucy, my dear !
SACKETT (*looking left*).   There's another wood-nymph.
Re-enter MRS. VAN. L. 3. E.

MRS. VAN. Why, something must have happened.

SACKETT. It's an elderly wood-nymph--Eh ? By Jove,
it's Virginia's mother.

MRS. VAN. (going to LUCY). Why, the poor child has
fainted. Our carriage is at the foot of the hill—Oh, sir—if
you will run and get some water immediately.

SACKETT. Impossible, madame—1 am a doctor of medicine, and I cannot allow the lady to be removed from the
place in which she originally fell.

MRS VAN. I will go, then—you will be very careful of
her, doctor.

SACKETT. I shall give her the most devoted attention,
madam.

[*Exit* MRS. VAN. L. 3. E.

CARTER (*without* L.). Lucy, my dear Lucy (*entering* L. 2.
E.). Why, darling (*rushing to her*). My dear—dear girl—
I——

SACKETT (*pushing him away*). Will you oblige me, sir,
by keeping at a more respectful distance— don't you see the
lady needs air ? (*Aside*) This is the wood-nymph's papa !

CARTER. Well, sir—if it's all the same to you, sir, I will
take your place.

SACKETT. But it isn't all the same to me, sir. I am a
doctor of medicine, and the lady must not be removed from
the place in which she originally fell.

CARTER. But—confound it, sir, I am the lady's——

SACKETT. I understand, sir, you are the lady's father
(CARTER *turns away angrily*). Your anxiety is natural.
You will find a spring of cold water about a mile and a quar-
ter down the path in that direction—and—(*pointing* R. 2. E.)

CARTER. A mile and a quarter (*going* R. *stops*). I'll be
back in less than five minutes !

[*Exit hastily* R. 2. E. LUCY *recovers*.

LUCY (L.). Why—why, where am I ?

SACKETT. You are in the woods, my dear. But you are
still weak (*she tries to get up—he presses her back*). I don't
think it advisable to remove you from the place in which
you originally fell.

LUCY. But—but (*breaking from him, rising and going* L. C.)
Oh—I remember. There was a gun—then another gun——

SACKETT (*rising*). I beg your pardon—there was only one
gun ; the gun had two barrels. I was hunting for ducks.
As I reached this spot I discovered a very beautiful one—I
would say, a very beautiful young lady. I had barely time
to reach her—before she fell into my arms and——

LUCY. And you——

SACKETT. I allowed her to remain in the place where she
originally fell.

LUCY (*recognizing him*). Ah!

SACKETT. She recognizes me! You remember me, then?

LUCY. Oh yes, sir—I—I——

SACKETT (*eagerly, and throwing his arm around her waist*). We met but a moment, it is true, but a moment of such exquisite joy to me. I—I——

LUCY (*struggling*). Oh, sir—you mnsn't. It isn't right. I—I—am——

SACKETT. Since our first romantic meeting in the moonlight your image has been constantly before my eyes.

LUCY. Oh, sir—you musn't—I——

SACKETT. If I hadn't fallen in love with you, I should be a marble statue—If I did not express my love, I should be an Egyptian mummy—and if——

LUCY (*struggling*). Oh, sir, it isn't right, I say—It is very wrong—I—I am——

SACKETT. I know it, my dear, you are an angel (*tries to kiss her. Enter* CARTER. *He stops suddenly* R., *and coughs*), and by this hand I swear——

CARTER. Ahem!

SACKETT (*aside*). Egad! it's the old gentleman.

LUCY (*aside*). My husband!

SACKETT (*going to* CARTER). I say, my friend, didn't you make remarkably quick time to that spring of cold water and back?

CARTER (*sternly*). It's very evident, sir, that I didn't return too soon. I concluded I was a fool before I had gone ten rods. This is my——

SACK. Your daughter—I am very happy to——

LUCY. My husband.

CARTER (*snappishly*). Her husband, sir (SACKETT *recoils confusedly*).

SACKETT. Her husband, the devil! (*aside*). I don't wonder he wanted to take my place.

Re-enter MR. *and* MRS. VAN., *has pail of water,* L. 3. E.

MRS. VAN. Oh! my dear, you are better again.

SACKETT (*aside*). Hilio! Virginia's father (*sitting* C.)

VAN. How was it? Lucy, my dear, you must tell us all about it; how did it happen?

LUCY. Why—you see—I—I don't know much about it myself—b—but I heard a gun, and then I heard another gun,—

SACKETT (*rising*). I beg your pardon—there was only one gun—it had two barrels.

LUCY. And then I—I don't remember anything else, until I awoke and found myself in—in——

SACKETT. In the place in which she originally fell.

MRS. VAN. (*in* VAN.'s *ear*). She found herself in that gentleman's arms.

VAN. Ah !

MRS. VAN. And the gentleman being a doctor of medicine—

SACKETT. Yes—being a doctor of medicine—I was able to do what was best for her under the circumstances.

VAN. (*to* SACKETT). My dear sir, we owe you a deep debt of gratitude. Mr. Carter, I am sure, will never be able to express his obligation.

CARTER. Oh ! no. I can't express my gratitude.

VAN. And by-the-way, I hadn't thought of it before—my name is Vanderpool.

SACKETT. Eh ! Oh ! Ahem ! Yes—my name is—ah—(*aside*) what the devil is my name ? Virginia doesn't know I'm within two hundred miles of Saratoga—It won't do to tell the old gentleman my name—my name is—is—ah—

VAN. Your name is——

SACKETT (*with hesitation between the words*). Alphonso—della—Madonna—Martinetti.

CARTER. Alphonso—della—Ma—what ?

MRS. VAN. (*in* VAN.'s *ear*). His name is Alphonso della Madonna Martinetti.

VAN. Alphonso della ma who ? Oh—he's a foreigner.

SACK. I was born in sunny Italy.

VAN. You speak remarkably good English for a foreigner. Have you been long from home ?

SACK. Fate has consigned me to a life-long exile from my native land—and from the palaces of my ancestors.

CARTER. H'm—I suppose he's a prince in disguise.

Enter BENEDICT, L. 3. E.

LUCY (*aside*). Oh—I do so love princes in disguise !

BEN. Has anything happened ? I saw Mrs. Vanderpool running through the woods (*seeing* SACKETT). What—eh— why, my dear Bob (SACKETT *checks him*).

OMNES (*astonished*). " Bob !" (*general sensation*).

CARTER. He called the prince " Bob !"

MRS. VAN. Mrs. Benedict—your friend—his name is Alphonso della Madonna Martinetti—*Bob* ?

CARTER. Oh is it—*Bob*—Alphonso della Madonna Martinetti ?

LUCY. Perhaps it is Alphonso—Bob—della Martinetti.

BEN. Alphonso della Madonna Mar——

CARTER. Alphonso della Madonna Martinetti, that is the gentleman's name.

SACKETT. Ahem ! really I must explain. There is certainly some misunderstanding—my name is ———

MRS. VAN. (*in* VAN.'s *ear*). His name isn't Alphonso della Madonna Martinetti.

VAN. Eh ?—it isn't—what is it ?

MRS. VAN. His name is "*Bob.*"

VAN. "*Bob !*"

SACKETT. I—ah—ladies and gentlemen—I—I assure you that my name *is* Alphonso della Madonna Martinetti, but they call me "Bob"—for *short.*

LUCY. Ha, ha, ha, ha!

MRS. VAN. (*in* VAN.'s *ear*). They call him "Bob," for short.

VAN. Oh, his name is Bob Short?

CARTER. They call you Bob for short? That is a very remarkable concentration of syllables, sir.

BEN. I—I haven't the remotest idea of what you're all talking about—but (*aside to* BOB) I say, Bob, you may as well make a clean breast of it, whatever it is.

SACKETT (*resignedly*). Go on—drive ahead !

BEN. Ladies and gentlemen—allow me to introduce to you my warm personal friend and former schoolmate, Robert Sackett, Esq., Councillor and Attorney-at-Law, 121, Cedar Street, New York.

CARTER. Attorney-at-Law !

SACKETT (*pulling* BEN.'s *coat*). I'm a Doctor of Medicine, Jack.

CARTER (*savagely*). You will excuse me, Mr. Robert Sackett, but I do not see why it was absolutely necessary that a young lady who had fainted should continue to recline in the arms of an "Attorney-at-Law," when all her friends, including her husband, were anxious to relieve him of the burden.

SACKETT. I assure you, my dear sir, I tried to do what was best for the lady under the circumstances.

CARTER. The circumstances are exactly what I object to, sir. What the devil do you mean, sir, by assuring us at a critical moment that you were a *doctor* ?

SACKETT. My dear sir, I *was* a Doctor—a Doctor—of *Divinity* (*he bows to* LUCY, *she bowing low in return*).

CARTER. Damn your divinity, sir ! (*turns up stage angrily*).

LUCY. Oh, Mr. Carter ! (*following him up*).

Enter SIR MORT., L. 3 E., *with pillow under each arm, and loaded with blankets, &c.*

SIR MORTIMER. Mrs. Vanderpool, I have obeyed your instructions—I entered the farm-house, and I captured two pillows, a sheet, and a blanket before the proprietors fully understood the nature of my errand.

Enter WETHERTREE, L. 2. E., *with pitcher in one hand, large
basket in the other, carriage cushion under each arm—
looks* R *and* L.

WETH. Mrs. Vanderpool, I've obeyed your instructions to
the letter—I've brought all the carriage cushions. and a
pitcher of water, and the basket (*sees* SACKETT). Who the
devil is that? I've seen that face before (*goes up* L.).

SACKETT. There's another wood nymph.

SIR MOR. (*staring at* SACKETT). I've seen that face before
(*goes up* R.).

SACKETT. Here's a pair of wood nymphs!

Enter VIRGINIA *and* LITTLEFIELD, R. 2. C.

VIRG. (*seeing* ROBERT). Robert!

SACKETT. Oh, Lord—Virginia!

VIRG. My *dear* Robert! (*runs to him quickly*, R. C.

EVERYBODY. Her "*dear* Robert!"

VIRG. What a delightful surprise!

SACKETT. Delightful!

VAN. (*confused and anxious*). Ahem!—ah, I say, old lady,
ahem—ah—Virginia—Mr. Sackett——

SACKETT. My darling Virginia! (*To* VAN.) I owe you an
apology, Mr. Vanderpool, and Mrs. Vanderpool. I have
long loved your daughter in secret.

LITTLEFIELD (R., *excitedly*). He has long loved her in
secret!

SACKETT. And her timid blushes confess, sir, that she has
returned my love.

LITTLEFIELD. She has returned his love!

SACKETT. And now, sir, I throw myself at your feet.
I——

EFFIE *enters* L. U. E.

EFFIE. What's all the fuss about. anyway? what's the
row? (*sees* ROBERT) Ah, Robert! (*runs to him*) *My* dear
Robert!

EVERYBODY (*walking up and down stage, excitedly*). *Her*
dear Robert!

EFFIE. Ah, dear Robert, I didn't know you were in Saratoga.

VIRG. Your dear Robert?—he is my dear Robert.

EFFIE. Your —

VIRG. Yes, mine; he is my——; he has sworn a dozen
times——

EFFIE. Your——sworn. Ha! I see it all!—the perjured
wretch! (*goes up and down stage, furiously, followed by* SIR
MORT. *and* WETH.).

VIRG. I see it all, sir!—your vows are worthless, sir!
(*goes up and down stage, followed by* LITTLEFIELD).

SACKETT (*seizing* BEN *down* C.). My dear Jack, if any one finds a body floating in the lake—or a pistol-ball through the head—or prussic-acid in the stomach—please identify it, and have it decently buried (*starts* R. 2. E., *stops, and staggers back* C.).

Enter MRS. ALSTON, R. 2. C.

MRS. ALSTON (R. C.). Ah, my dear Robert!

ALL. Her dear Robert!

CARTER. Egad! he's everybody's dear Robert!

SACKETT (*reeling to* BEN.). I say, Benedict, there's **my** *widow!*

BEN. Your widow!—the devil it is! That's *my* widow! (*pushes him off, and rushes up and down stage furious;* EFFIE, VIRG., *and others walk up and down as before*).

SACK. (*to* CARTER). My venerable friend, support me. (CARTER *starts off up and down stage indignantly*). Ladies and gentlemen, please allow me to remain in the place in which I originally fell. (*Drops on stage,* C. WETH. *and* SIR MORT. *throw blankets and sheets on him, which they have carried up to this time. Everybody going up and down stage in a most excited manner*).

CURTAIN.

ACT IV.

SCENE.—*Parlours of the Grand Union, Saratoga, elegantly furnished and upholstered. Table,* C., *and two chairs, sofas,* R. *and* L. OLD REM. *discovered sitting* R. *of table, fanning himself; newspaper in his hand.*

OLD REM. (*grumbling*). Waiter! they call this travelling for pleasure, h—m!—travelling for pleasure—waiter! travelling—for—waiter!!

Enter GYP, L. C., *fanning himself.*

GYP (R. *of* OLD REM.). Possibly I can do suffin for **you,** **sah**!

OLD REM. Possibly you can.

GYP. Did you call for a culled gem'men, sah?

OLD REM. Bring me some Congress water.

GYP (L.). Oh, yes, sah!—ahem! certainly, sah—ahem! (*standing still*).

OLD REM. Well, do you propose bringing it this summer or next?

GYP. Beg pardon, sah, but we culled gemmen at Saratoga have made a new rule, sah—we always take it in advance now, sah.

OLD REM. Oh, you always take it in advance now (*gives him currency*).

Enter MUFFINS *and children up stage.* MUFFINS *gives the children water from silver pitcher up* R.

GYP (*going—stops*). Beg pardon, sah, but this is a ragged one, sah ; we culled gemmen of Saratoga have made a new rule, sah !

OLD REM. M—m. I am sorry to have put a coloured gentleman to so much trouble (*gives him another*). There ! take that, you rascal, and bring me some Congress water. (*Exit* GYP, L. C.). Ahem ! they call this travelling for pleasure !

LITTLE BOY. Where is mamma to-day, Muffins ?

MUFFINS. Your mother is at the races, my darling.

LITTLE GIRL. We have hardly seen mamma at all since yesterday morning. Where was mamma last night, when we were going to bed ?

MUFFINS (*coming down*). Getting ready for the ball.

LITTLE GIRL. And where is papa, Muffins ?

MUFFINS. Your father is at the races, too.

LITTLE BOY. Where was papa last night ?

MUFFINS. Where was your father last night ? I don't know any more about that than your mother does, my darling. What uncomfortable questions these children do ask, to be sure !   [*Exit with children*, L. 2. E.

OLD REM. Travelling for pleasure ! A man might as well be in a brick oven, with a warming-pan under his feet, and call it "travelling for pleasure" (*going* C.). Whew ! (GYP, *entering, runs against* OLD REM., *who pushes him aside*). Get out of my way, rascal—do !   [*Exit*, R. C.

GYP (*indignantly*). That individual is wantin' in proper respeck for culled gentility. De gemmen what is in good humour at Saratoga gives me fifty cents, and say, "Gyp, you rascal, go and take a drink ;" and de gemmen what isn't in good humour say, "Gyp, you rascal, get out of my way, you rascal !" We culled gemmen at Saratoga is rascals, whichever way you put it.   [*Exit* GYP, R. 1. E.

C. *Enter* VIRGINIA, *rapidly, as if just from her carriage, followed by* FRANK LITTLEFIELD. *She is nervous and angry.*

LITTLEFILD. I'll do anything for your sake, my darling Virginia—scale the Alps—find the North Pole—

VIRGINIA (*walking back and forth angrily*). I don't want the North Pole.

LITTLEFIELD. Pierce the deep empyrean of the vaulted arch—

VIRGINIA. I don't want you to pierce the deep empyrean of the vaulted arch.

LITTLEFIELD. Meet the tiger in his secret lair—

VIRGINIA (R.). Oh, you needn't fight the tiger on my account.

THE MAJOR (*strolling in quietly*, L. 1. E.). The tiger!—that interests me. Mr. Vanderpool is excited (*up* L, *quietly*).

VIRGINIA. Frank Littlefield, if your professions of love for me are true——

LITTLEFIELD (L. *raising his hand as if to swear*). True—I—

VIRGINIA (R.). If you have one spark of honourable manhood——

LITTLEF. Manhood!—I swear——

VIRGINIA (L.). If—if—— Challenge Robert Sackett to mortal combat!

THE MAJOR. There's been a row; this is particularly interesting—1 will offer my own services.

LITTLEFIELD (L.). I will, Virginia. If he refuse to fight—

VIRGINIA. Post him for a coward!

LITTLEFIELD. I will. If he do not refuse –

VIRGINIA (*anxiously*). Oh, but he *will*, Frank. I'm sure he will refuse.

LITTLEFIELD. If he do not refuse—I take my life in my hand—too happy—only too happy to lay it down in such a cause as that.   [*Exit, with impressive steps* L.

VIRG. (*looking after him*). If—if Robert Sackett should accept the challenge—perhaps—I—Frank—Frank—

THE MAJOR (*walking down* R). Miss Vanderpool—I beg your pardon—no intention of listening, I assure you—but—you mentioned the "tiger," just now; that word attracted my attention. I am somewhat familiar with the tiger—in fact, I have had many honourable scars;—you also mentioned Mr. Sackett's name.

VIRGINIA (L.). (*putting her foot*). I did. Mr. Robert Sackett has most grossly insulted me.

THE MAJOR. Indeed—allow me the privilege—Miss Virginia.

VIRGINIA. You will challenge Robert Sackett? (*Drawing up.*) Do it!

THE MAJOR. Your servant, Miss Virginia (*raises her hand and going* L. E.). (*Aside*) Two millions—and the only daughter. I have taken greater risks than that for smaller stakes.   [*Exit* L. 1. E.

VIRGINIA. So—so—Mr. Robert Sackett!—we shall see (*going up* L., *where she walks back and forth nervously*).

Enter EFFIE *rapidly up* C., *followed by* WETH. *and* SIR MORTIMER, EFFIE *stops abruptly down* L., WETH. *and* SIR M. *stumble over each other, she then walks* R. *and* L. *excitedly, followed by the gentlemen who stumble over each other as she turns abruptly at each end.*

WETH. But, Miss Effie——

SIR MORT. Miss—a—eh—Miss Ef-fie——

WETH. (*to* SIR MORT. *at one end of the walk*). Get out of my way, sir—(*to* EFFIE)—Miss Effie——

SIR MORT. (*at other end of walk*). I beg your pardon—will you keep out of the way ?—(*to* MISS EFFIE)—a—h—Miss Ef—fie——

> [*Each time they meet they draw up and glare at each other.*

WETH. (*at one end*). Confound it—sir ! (*they draw up*). My dear Miss—— (L.).

SIR MORT. (R.) (*at other end*). Dear me, sir ! (*they draw up*). My charming Miss——

EFFIE (R., *seizing* SIR MORTIMER'S *wrist and coming up suddenly with the air of a tragedy queen*). Sir Mortimer Muttonleg (*breathing heavily and looking over her shoulder at* WETHERTREE). I will speak with you presently, Mr. Cornelius Wethertree (WETHERTREE *walks* L.). Sir Mortimer Muttonleg, a word with you in private. You say you are my slave—that—was —your—language—I be-lieve.

SIR MORT. Y-e-s—allow me—to assure—you—a—h— Miss Effie ——

EFFIE. On one condition— I will be yours—*for ever.*

SIR MORT. My dear Miss Effie—I am sure—a-h—you delight me, upon my honour—you do. Name the condition —I shall be only too happy to——

EFFIE (*impressively*). Challenge Mr. Robert Sackett to mortal combat (SIR MORTIMER *falls back* R. *into chair*, EFFIE *crosses with tragical manner to* WETHERTREE L.—*seizes his wrist suddenly—he starts*). Mr. Cornelius Wethertree—a word with you in private. You say you are my slave :—that —was—your—language—I—be-lieve.

WETHERTREE. Your most devoted slave, Miss Effie—I ——

EFFIE. On one condition— I will be yours—for ever.

WETHERTREE. My dear Miss Effie (*eagerly*), any condition in the world—I shall be delighted to——

EFFIE. Challenge Mr. Robert Sackett to mortal combat.

> [WETHERTREE *falls back* L., EFFIE *swings up* C. *with a majestic stride.*

SIR MORT. (*aside*). Challenge— Mr.—Robert—Sackett— to—the—deuce—you know !

WETHERTREE (*aside*). Challenge—Mr. Robert—Sackett —-to mortal—combat !

> [EFFIE *moves down* C. *with the same grand air.*

EFFIE (C.). Gentlemen !—I have spoken :—it is enough. Retire.

WETH. (*aside*). I wonder if there is any danger of Sackett's accepting a challenge.   [*Exit* L. 1. E.

SIR MORT. These American girls are the most unaccount-
able creatures.
[*Exit* R. 1. E. EFFIE *swings up* R., *where she moves
to and fro.*
Enter CARTER, R. 1. E., *rapidly, very angry—followed by*
LUCY.
LUCY. My dear—husband—will you listen to me, this is
madness.
CARTER (*walking* R. *and* L. *front excitedly*). I say, I shall
insist on satisfaction.
LUCY. You have been growing more and more furious—
every step of the way home.
CARTER. And I shall continue to grow more and more
furious until I have the satisfaction due to a gentleman—a
dozen warm kisses—madam.
LUCY. He did not know I was married.
CARTER. A doctor of divinity, madam !
LUCY. He took the best possible care of me.
CARTER. Exactly—the place in which you originally fell,
madam ! Alphonso della Madonna Martinetti—*Bob*, ma-
dam !
FREDERIC *appears* R. 1. E. ; *cane in hand, eye-
glasses, &c.*
FREDERIC. Hillo ! the governor is excited.
CARTER. Mr. Robert Sackett, attorney at law, Cedar
Street, New York—has insulted my wife—madam ! I am a
gentleman of the old school—I shall insist upon satisfaction
(*moves about nervously*).
FREDERIC. Eh?—oh—Mr. Robert Sackett has insulted
—our wife ? (CARTER *stops suddenly—stares at* FRED.). Cer-
tainly—we shall insist upon satisfaction.
[CARTER *walks across to* FREDERIC, R., *takes him by
the ear and leads him across and out* L. 1. E.
CARTER. I should really like to know exactly whose wife
this is.   [*Exit* L. 1. E.
LUCY (*turning up stage*). Oh ! girls ! here you are.
EFFIE. Yes—we are here.
[*Coming down* R., *with a provoked air;* VIRG. *comes
down* L.
LUCY (C.). Did you hear Mr. Carter?
VIRG. Yes—we heard Mr. Carter (*with petulant air*).
LUCY (C.). He was furious all the way home—I thought
he would kill the poor horses. Mr. Carter is a gentleman of
the old school ; he insists on demanding satisfaction of Mr.
Robert Sackett.
VIRGINIA. Good for Carter !
EFFIE. Hurrah ! for a gentleman of the old school !

LUCY. Have you seen anything more of Robert Sackett?

EFFIE. No, I haven't seen anything more of Mr. Robert Sackett—and I don't want to see anything more of Mr. Robert Sackett—except his funeral.

LUCY. If he's in Saratoga—I must find him—I will look for him everywhere.

EFFIE. Yes, you are anxious to find the place in which you originally fell, I suppose. I know all about that sort of thing—I've been there.

VIRG. So have I—I know how it is myself.

LUCY. Oh! do not quarrel with me now—I am wretched. Girls, girls—you do not know the feelings of a wife.

EFFIE. No—and we're not likely to know them, as long as you can help it.

VIRG. That's what we're so mad about.

LUCY. I *must* find Mr. Sackett—I will beg of him—I will insist—I—I—I must find Mr. Sackett!   [*Exit* C. D. L.

EFFIE. Virginia!

VIRGINIA. Effie! (*They kiss and entwine arms*).

EFFIE. Let's go up into your room—and lock the door and have a good cry—all to ourselves.

VIRGINIA. Yes! (*half sobbing*), we'll get on the bed—and we'll shut the blinds—and we'll—we'll——

EFFIE (*suddenly drawing up*). No—we won't—no, we won't. We won't do anything of the kind.

VIRG. Why—wh—what else can we girls do under circumstances like this?

EFFIE. I'll tell you what we'll do :—we won't let anybody know we care anything about it—we'll go and get dressed—and we'll come down into the drawing-room, exactly as if nothing had happened, and we'll talk and flirt and smile and look pretty, and say silly things to the gentlemen, just as we girls always do at Saratoga.   [*Exeunt arm in arm*, C.D.

Enter MRS. ALSTON. L. 1. E., *followed by* BENEDICT.

BENEDICT (L.). But, my dear madam !—

MRS. ALSTON. Very well—Mr. Benedict—very well. You have my ultimatum, Mr. Robert Sackett has grossly insulted me—if you really love me, as you say you do, and are a *man*, as you profess to be by your clothes—you will demand an explanation.

BEN. But, my dear Olivia——

MRS. ALSTON. Don't call me your "dear Olivia," sir, until you have taken satisfaction—in some form—of Mr. Robert Sackett.

BEN. But Bob is my bosom friend.

MRS. ALSTON. Oh, very well, sir ; if you would rather have Mr. Sackett as a "bosom friend" than myself, you are welcome to the choice.

BEN. He has been my companion.

MRS. ALSTON. *If you* prefer Mr. Robert Sackett as a " companion "——

BEN. My classmate in college—my crony—

MRS. ALSTON. *If you* prefer Robert Sackett as a " crony."

BEN. My room-mate.

MRS. ALSTON. If you prefer Mr. Robert Sackett as a— ahem—

BEN. The code of honour belongs to the middle ages.

MRS. ALSTON. The grand old. middle ages—when men were men—and women had protectors.

BEN. Civilization, madam !—the code of honour is a relic of barbarism.

MRS. ALSTON. A little more middle age barbarity and a little less " modern civilization ' would improve the " gentlemen " of Saratoga.

BEN. (L.). I should be making a fool of myself.

MRS. ALSTON. Your friends might not fail to recognize you on that account.

BEN. I—I might, perhaps, punch Bob's head.

MRS. ALSTON. Oh—very well—if modern civilization will allow you to " punch " the young man's head—do it by all means.

BEN. But, my dear Olivia—I don't think Bob would—in fact—it's ten to one he will cheerfully resign all claim upon yourself to me—and——

MRS. ALSTON. Indeed—indeed! So I am to be passed from one owner to the next like a thoroughbred race-horse—after the races are over. I'm to be bargained for and delivered—according to contract—my good points guaranteed—warranted sound—sold and delivered free of charges—halter—blanket—and harness to go with the animal.

[*Exit angrily*, R. 1. E.

Enter SACKETT, L. 1. E.

BEN. (*without seeing* SACKETT, *who is looking out cautiously at the various entrances*). Confoundedly awkward for me—the widow is as peremptory about her orders as a colonel of a regiment on dress-parade.

SACK. Jack.

BEN. You here, Bob—

SACK. I—am—here—staunch and true—as the fellow says in the " Duke's Motto "—The affairs of my—my heart—have arrived at such a peculiar crisis—I consider it necessary as an American gentleman—to be on the spot. If I should retire to my suburban residence under the present circumstances —it would appear like an ignominious retreat. I am here to meet the enemy—provided, of course, it doesn't come in the shape of female petticoats (*looking* R. *and* L.)—I shall avoid the enemy in that shape—if 1 have to run for it.

BEN. Bob!—I have been commissioned by Mrs. Olivia Alston—to punch your head.

SACK. Do it, Benedict ;—my head is entirely at your disposal ; punch it by all means, I am a penitent and contrite man. I never saw a head which could be punched, with so much satisfaction to its owner, as mine, at the present moment. Punch my head by all means.

BEN. Seriously, Bob—the widow——

SACK. As I told you on a former occasion—the widow was an accident—I yield all claim, title, and interest in that direction, to yourself.

BEN. Oh, 1 know you would do that—it's all right, Jack, so far as you and I are concerned—but Mrs. Alston—

SACK. The widow insists on the technical points in the case :—she wants the flag saluted. That's all right—we can manage that, Jack.

BEN. Manage it—Bob—do you really think I'd better punch your head ?

SACK. N-o ! On the whole—I—I've thought of a more convenient arrangement.

BEN. Oh—it's perfectly convenient, Bob,—to me. You needn't—hesitate on that account.

SACK. I don't.

BEN. The widow won't consent to anything less than that, you know.

SACK. She shall have more. What is the number of your room ?

BEN. No. 73—private parlour, with bedroom and bath-room attached.

Enter GYP, R. 1. E., *with salver and note.*

GYP. Mr. Robert Sackett, I believe, sah.

SACK. I believe so.

GYP. Yes—sah—gem-man pointed you out. He requested me to present dis note, sah—very important, sah—

SACK. (*reading address*). "Robert Sackett, Esq."—that's all right.

GYP. Beg pardon, sah, but we culled gem-man—at Sara-toga—has made a new rule—sah—we takes postage at bof ends, now, sah !

SACK. Oh ! I wasn't aware of the new regulation in the post-office department (*gives him something ;* GYP *walks up* R., *s'ops*)—the franking privilege has never existed at Sara-toga. (*To* BENEDICT)—I say—Jack—I'll meet you in your room, No. 73—in fifteen minutes. We'll make it all right with the widow. I have a plan that will work to perfection

—get you out of this scrape, and me, too,—and the widow more than satisfied. In the meantime—find the widow— tell her you have challenged me to mortal combat. I accepted eagerly. Place, your room—time, immediate— coffee for two—pistols—and all that sort of thing.

BEN. I will—Bob—admirable. Ha—ha—ha—the widow will think we're perfect savages ! Ha, ha, ha, Captain Jack was a Christian—compared with us, and the Spaniards ! human beings—I'll tell her—Bob,—I'll tell her—pistols— coffee—revenge ! Ha, ha, ha ! [*Exit* R. 1. E.

SACK. (*following him up and speaking*, R.). And, I say, Jack—bid the widow a last farewell before you leave her— and don't forget to kiss her a dozen times or so—on my account—(*turning* L.)—I've overdrawn my account already, by-the-way, in that direction—but the bank has a remark- ably strong capital.

GYP (*aside*). Coffee—and pistols—room No. 73—dare's sumpin wrong—goin on ! shuah !

SACK. (*reading address of note*). "Robert Sackett, Esq." (*opening it, sees* GYP)--Well—anything more—no more post- age due—this is only single weight—I believe —

GYP. De gem-man tole me to wait for de answer—sah—

SACK. Ah—(*reading*). Here it comes. "Robert Sackett, Esq." "I have been requested by Miss Virginia Vanderpool" —(*reads signature*)—"Frank Littlefield." Say to Mr. Frank Littlefield—that Mr. Robert Sackett will be pleased to meet him—let me see (*looks at his watch*)—it's now just six o'clock —I shall be pleased to meet the gentleman at—where the deuce shall I meet him ? Oh, certainly—at private parlour —No. 73—at half-past six pre-cisely.

GYP. Yes—sah.

SACK. Jack may be a little surprised—but he always did like company (*turning to* GYP, *who is deliberately going* R. 3. E.). General Washington - bring me a glass of Congress water (*exit* GYP). It is a trifle warm to-day--or else I am getting excited.

Enter 1ST COLOURED WAITER, R. 1. E.

1ST WAIT. Mistah Sackett.

SACK. That's my name.

1ST WAIT. Gem'man— sah—note, sah—very 'tickler, sah.

SACK. (*taking note*). "Robert Sackett, Esq." (*hands waiter something*), there's the postage—(*reads*) "Cornelius Wether- tee"—conduct as a gentleman—insult—explanation—Miss Effie Remington—the devil !—say to Mr. Cornelius Wether- ree that Mr. Robert Sackett will be happy to meet him—at private parlour, No. 73, at half-past six precisely.

1ST WAIT. Yes—sah (*going*).

SACK. Commodore Perry (*waiter pauses*), bring me a glass of claret.

1ST WAIT. Yes, sah. [*Exit*, L. 1. E.

SACK. I feel warmer—this is growing interesting.

Enter 2ND WAITER, R. 1. E.

2ND WAIT. Mistah Sackett?

SACK. That's my name.

2ND WAIT. Gem'man, sah—note, sah—very 'tickler, sah.

SACK. By Jove, I'm getting out of postage—(*hands him something ; takes note*). "Robert Sackett, Esq.," " Sir Mortimer Muttonleg"—what the deuce has Sir Mortimer to—eh?—"Miss Effie Remington,"—by Jove, she's a little tigress; she's set two of them on me. Say to Sir Mortimer Muttonleg that Mr. Robert Sackett will be happy to meet him at private parlour, No. 73, at half-past six precisely.

2ND WAIT. (*going*). Yes, sah.

SACK. Ah, Andrew Jackson—(*waiter stops*)--a glass o. Bourbon whiskey straight !

2ND WAIT. Yes, sah. [*Exit*, R. 1. E.

SACK. It is becoming warmer and warmer. Let me see – Effie—Virginia—the widow—(*counting on his fingers*)—if they average two apiece, the chances of my passing a comfortable night are not flattering.

Enter 3RD WAITER, L. 1. E.

3RD WAIT. Mistah Sackett, sah?

SACK. I am becoming more and more strongly convinced, sir, that that is my name.

3RD WAIT. Gem'man, sah—note, sah—very 'tickler, sah.

SACK. (*taking note, and looking sharply at waiter, who is grinning at him*). No, sir—no, sir. You have come to the wrong man—(*turning away*)—I am willing to be *shot* by the entire party ; but damn me if I pay any more postage on these miserable notes--(*reading*). Hello?— " William Carter," "my wife,"—I didn't count her ; the man that wrote that meant blood at every stroke of the pen. (*To waiter*) Bring me a glass of brandy-and-water—no sugar.

3RD WAIT. (*going*). Yes, sah.

SACK. And—ah—Ulysses (*waiter stops*), say to the Honourable Wm. Carter that I shall be happy to meet his wife—at private parlour—I mean, his wife will be happy to meet me—I would say, the Hon Wm. Carter—No. 73—half-past six—get out—(*exit* 3*rd Wait.*, L. 1. E.). Egad ! we're likely to have quite a party at private parlour No. 73 (*going* R. 1. E.). Thank heaven, I'm through with them now !

Enter 4TH WAITER, R. 1. E.

4TH WAIT. Mr. Sackett, sah?

[SACKETT *turns, looks at him, leans on the back of a chair deliberately.*

SACK. Did you address me, General Sherman ?

4TH WAIT. Yes, sah.

SACK. What was the nature of your remark ? I may have misunderstood it.

4TH WAIT. Your name is Sackett, I believe, sah ?

SACK. (C.). Sackett—Sackett ? (*taking the four notes from his pocket, spreads them out in one hand like a pack of cards*) — I am under the impression that I have seen that name somewhere.

4TH WAIT. Gem'man, sah—note, sah--very 'tickler, sah.

SACKETT *walks across, takes note, opens it deliberately with his penknife.*

SACK. (*reading*). "Robert Sackett, Esq.   Sir,—You have been making love,"—the gentleman is correct : I *have* been making love—" to "—hello ! what's this ?   " You have been making love—to—my—mother !" (*To waiter*) Senator, that note is not for me (*folding the note, and handing it back*). There are some things in the way of making love, which even a gentleman can't stoop to. I have never yet been guilty of making love to another man's mother (*walking L., and speaking with the air of a man uttering a weighty moral precept*).

4TH WAIT. Must be for you, sah ; de young gem'man pointed you out personably, sah.

SACKETT *walks back, takes the note.*

SACK. (*reading*). "Frederick Augustus Carter." Ah, yes ; exactly.   General Sheridan, you may bring me a glass of—ice-water.

4TH WAIT. Yes, sah.   [*Exit, R. 1. E.*

SACK. If Mr. Frederick Augustus Carter should happen to come into private parlour, No. 73, I shall recall to his memory the tender ministrations of his first mother ; the young man needs a spanking.

Re-enter GYP, C. R.

GYP. Glass Congress water, sah.

SACK. Eh ? oh, yes—I forgot.

Re-enter 1ST WAITER, L. 1. E.

1ST WAIT. Glass claret, sah.   [*Stands left of* GYP.

Re-enter 2ND WAITER, R. 1. E.

2ND WAIT. Bourbon whiskey straight, sah.

[*Moves to* R. *of* GYP.

Re-enter 3RD WAITER, L. 1. E.

3RD WAIT. Brandy-and-water, sah—no sugar.

[*Moves to* L. *of* 1ST WAITER.

Re-enter 4TH WAITER, L. 3. E.

4TH WAIT. Glass ice-water, sah.

[*Takes his place beside* 3RD WAITER.

SACKETT *stares at each as he enters, and finally stands before the row, his back to the audience, looking from one end of the line to the other.*

SACK. (*turning to audience*). The situation calls for a speech. (*Turns to them*) Fellow American citizens—

ALL WAITERS. Ya, ha! ya, ha! (*grinning and recovering themselves*).

SACK. Of African descent.

Enter MAJOR LUDDINGTON WHIST, L. 1. E.

MAJOR. Mr. Sackett—

SACK. Eh? oh—one moment, major. Gentlemen, you will oblige me by taking it all to room No. 73. Left face! forward—file right—march!—file left!—double quick! (*The waiters flank and march according to orders out* L. 2. E.) Now, my dear major, I am at your service.

EFFIE *steps in, sees* SACKETT, *starts with a quick* "Ah!" *and stands motionless.*

EFFIE. There is the perfidious wretch himself!

SACK. (*aside*). If Major Luddington Whist comes on a similar errand, it means serious work. I wonder if Effie Remington has set him on me, too? I have heard that (*aloud*) you wish to see me, major?

MAJOR (L.). On a very delicate matter, Mr. Sackett. A young lady—

EFFIE (*aside*). Oh, dear! Virginia set the major on him —that means business.

SACK. I understand you perfectly. Allow me to say, my dear major—in all seriousness—that I am ready to meet you anywhere, at any time, and with any weapon you care to name. If you choose to dispute with me the right to Miss Effie Remington's affections, I am entirely at your service.

EFFIE. Ah! seems to be in earnest now.

SACK. Whatever may be the feelings of that lady, for myself I shall defend my own interest in her against all comers, until I receive a formal dismissal from her own lips.

EFFIE. The darling fellow!

MAJOR (L.). Really, there is a mistake. You will excuse me, Mr. Sackett, but we are labouring under a misunderstanding. The young lady to whom I refer is Miss Virginia Vanderpool.

SACK. Oh, Virginia Van——that's a very different thing.

EFFIE. A different thing! Oh,—il est charmant!

MAJOR. Not so different, I trust, that you will refuse the satis——

SACK. Certainly not. Only I had fully resolved in the other case to carve you limb from limb. Meet me in private parlour—No. 73—at half-past six : will that be agreeable to yourself ?

MAJOR. Perfectly so ; au revoir, Mr. Sackett.

SACK. Da—da ! a bottle or two of Roderer, major ?

THE MAJOR. Moet et Chandon is my favourite.

SACK. Very well—Moet et Chandon—(THE MAJOR *bows and exits* L. 1. E.)—Ten minutes after six—(*looking at his watch*)— let me see—I must not forget that I have an engagement at half-past six. [*Going* R. 1. E.

EFFIE (*hurrying forward*). Robert—Mr. Sackett.

SACK (*turning, sees* EFFIE—*hesitates—bows*). Good-afternoon, Miss Remington. [*He turns to go* R. 2. E.

Enter GYP, R. 2. E., *appearing suddenly.*

. GYP. Mistah Sackett.

SACK. Private parlour—number seventy-three—half-past six—whoever it is. [*Exit* R. 1. E.

EFFIE. Robert (*moving to* R. 1. E.)—Robert !

Enter MRS. ALSTON *rapidly* R. 1. E.

MRS. ALSTON. Oh ! Effie !

Enter VIRGINIA *rapidly.*

VIRGINIA. Oh—Effie—Mrs. Alston——

Enter LUCY L. 2. E. *rapidly.*

LUCY. Effie—Virginia—Mrs. Alston !

EFFIE. Oh—Virginia—Lucy—Olivia !

[*Ladies moving to and fro.*

MRS. ALSTON. Oh—Jack—my dear Jack—my first love !
[*Sinks into a chair* C.

VIRGINIA. Frank—my last love ! [*Sinks beside her* L.

LUCY. My husband ! [*Sinks beside her* R.

EFFIE (*standing back of her chair* C.). ROBERT !! j'aime—que toi—my *only* love !

[*Ladies all choke, and then burst into simultaneous sobs.*
Picture.

CURTAIN.

END OF ACT FOURTH.

ACT V.

SCENE.—*Private parlour, Number 73. Handsomely furnished. Doors* R. 2. E. *and* L. C. *back. A large wardrobe or dresser at back* C. *Entrance door*, L. 3. E. *Table* C., *with open pistol-cases ; box of cigars. Tray of champayne and cooler, pitcher, &c.*

Discovered at rise of curtain, BENEDICT *arranging things on table.*

BENEDICT. Ha—ha—ha !— I've fixed it so far with the

widow; she thinks I've challenged Bob—and we're going to
fight—ha—ha—and when Bob comes he'll tell me his plan—
I can't imagine how he proposes to carry the thing out—but
trust Bob Sackett for that—I never was good in matters of
this kind—they're out of the regular line. I've got the pistols all right (*blowing through them*). No balls there. I
wonder what Bob proposes to do. And the champagne—ha
—ha—ha! We'll have a jolly time at all events. (*Knock.*)
Come in (*Opens the door. Enter* GYP, *followed by all the
other waiters, with their salver and tumblers. They stop in
line up stage*). Eh—what the deuce!

GYP. Congress water, sah.

1*st* WAIT. Claret, sah.

2*nd* WAIT. Bourbon whiskey straight, sah.

3*rd* WAIT. Brandy and water, sah—no sugar.

4*th* WAIT. Ice water, sah.

[*They all put down their tumbler and fall back to line.*

BEN. Well, what the deuce——

SACK. (*entering* L. 2. E.). Here I am, Jack. Hello—you
have company, I see.

BEN. I - should—say—I—had. Where the deuce did
they come from?

SACK. All right, Jack—It's only my bodyguard. Here
you are, King William (*gives* GYP *a bill*), divide that with
the rest of the army. Left face, forward, march!

[*They march out* L. GYP *hesitates at door.*

GYP. Suffin's up heah—sartin. Gem'men doesn't have
pistols and dem tings all for nuffin. Suffin's wrong up in dis
heah room—sartin. I'll tell somebody, shuah. [*Exit* L. 2. E.

BEN. Well—now, Bob, tell me the rest of your plan. The
widow is all right. She understands that I have demanded
satisfaction of you, and that you have accepted the challenge.

SACK. (R.). Very well. The rest of the plan is the simplest
thing in the world. In the first place—you, of course,
haven't the least desire to shoot me.

BEN. Certainly not.

SACK. And I haven't the least desire that you should. I
say, Benedict, you are certain there aren't any bullets in
these pistols?

BEN. Not a chamber in either of them would kill a fly on
the wall at two paces.

SACK. Good. I haven't the least objection to what they
call the "smell of powder." It isn't the smell of powder I
object to; it's the bullets. As I was about to say—I will
take one of these pistols. I will put a ball in it, and I will
shoot you in the arm or leg—or anywhere else you choose—
do you see?

BEN. No. I don't think I do see it.

SACK. Simplest thing in the world. I shoot you in the arm or leg; you send for a surgeon; dangerously wounded, you know. Mrs. Alston hears that you have risked your life in defence of her honour; she flies to your bedside, nurses you through a fever, and marries you as soon as you get out of your room. Nothing could be simpler.

BEN. Yes—the plan is certainly simple enough.

SACK. You may lose an arm or a leg, my dear fellow; but you will gain a widow. I speak as a friend, Benedict, interested in your happiness, and willing to do anything that will tend to that result.

BEN. (*rising*). Yes, my dear Bob. Your friendship affects me to tears.

SACK. Don't mention it, old boy. Twenty minutes after six; it is nearly time for my numerous guests to make their appearance;—by-the-way, Benedict—I have taken a slight liberty. I have no room as yet in Saratoga. I asked a friend who has a grievance in connection with these recent little female affairs of mine—to drop in here at half-past six.

BEN. Oh—certainly—the room is entirely at your disposal.

SACK. In fact—I—I asked several friends to come in. I didn't keep track of the exact number. It did occur to me that it might surprise you a little – but——

BEN. My dear Jack—I assure you that nothing in the world that you might do would surprise me in the least. (*Knock* L. 3. E.) There's one of your "friends" now.

[*Knock again.*

SACK. He seems determined to be in time—I say, Benedict, if you'll retire to——

BEN. Certainly. This is your affair—only if you need my assistance, Bob——

SACK. I shall certainly call upon you.

[BENEDICT *exits* L. 2. E. *Knock.*

SACK. (*opening door*). Walk in, sir.

Enter quickly MRS. CARTER, *with opera cloak* L. 2. E.

SACK. (*starting back*). Eh? (*she throws back her cloak*) Mrs. Carter.

LUCY. (R.). Oh! Mr. Sackett. I know all.

SACKETT (L.). Mrs. Carter knows all.

LUCY. Mr. Carter has challenged you to mortal combat (*sees pistols*), pistols; four pistols! Mr. Sackett,—my dear Mr. Sackett.

SACK. (*aside*). "Dear Mr. Sackett,"—this is positively enchanting, to have a lovely woman like this so anxious for my personal safety.

Lucy. I have sought your room at the risk of my reputa·
tion—Oh! sir, for my sake, if not for your own—do not.

Sack. " For her sake "—these women are angels. For
your sake, Mrs. Carter, I would do anything (*taking her
hand*). My dear madam, you need have no further apprehen-
sion; your anxiety for my safety has touched my heart, but
I'm not in the least danger, I assure you.

Lucy (*coldly*). Sir,—Mr. Sackett,—I was not thinking of
you, sir.

Sack. (*drawing back*). Eh? oh!

Lucy. I was thinking of Mr. Carter, Mr. Carter's little
finger is dearer to me than your whole body, sir.

Sack. Why, the little fiend. (*Rapid knock* L. 2. E.) Hello!

Lucy. Oh! Mr. Sackett, my reputation—some one is
coming, conceal me somewhere—this room (*moving* R.)

Sackett (*confronting her*). No—there's a man in that room.

Lucy (*starting back*). A man!—oh somewhere—anywhere.

Sack. Here, into a wardrobe. (*Another knock* L. 2. E.) (*He
hurries her into wardrobe* C. *She drops opera cloak as she enters.*
Sack. *opens door.*) Come in, sir. (*Enter* Virginia *rapidly,
bonnet in hand.*) By Jove, another woman; Virginia.

Virg. Oh! Mr. Sackett, I came at the peril of my reputation to repair the evil I have done. I was hasty, foolish,
wicked this morning, but I'm not too late, say I'm not too
late.

Sack. Tears? Virginia is an angel. These women have
hearts after all. My darling Virginia (*goes to her, takes her
hand*). You, alone, of those whom I have loved—as man has
never loved woman before—you alone have shown a womanly
tenderness for my safety.

Virg. (*taking her hand away*). Your safety, Mr. Sackett.
Excuse me, sir—I—I was not thinking of *you.*

Sack. She wasn't thinking of me either!

Virg. I was thinking of Mr. Littlefield.

Sack. These women haven't any hearts at all.

Virg. Oh! Robert, Mr. Sackett—you will not meet Frank;
you will not risk a life that has become so dear to me. You
and I can be brother and sister, you know.

Sack. Y-e-s—and Frank Littlefield will be my brother-in-
law, I suppose.

Virg. Yes, you can be Frank's brother-in-law.

Sack. (*turning to her*). My darling sister.

Virg. Robert (*they embrace*).

Sack. Kiss your brother, my dear. (*Knock* L. 2. R.)

Virg. Why what was that? (*Knock.*) Somebody at the
door; oh, if it should be Frank! He'd never speak to me
again. Is there no other door? (*moving* R.)

SACK. (*confronting her*). Not in that room, my dear—there is a man in that room.

VIRG. A man. (*A knock.*) Oh, then I will hide in there (*going to wardrobe*).

SACK. No, not there either—Here—(*puts her in closet* L. C. *She drops her bonnet. Knock.* SACKETT *opens door*). Come in, sir. (*Enter* EFFIE *rapidly, she throws her scarf on chair*). Effie!

EFFIE. Robert!

SACK. Good-afternoon, Miss Remington. (*Aside*) I suppose *she* is anxious for somebody's personal safety. I shall certainly put in a bullet when I shoot at Mr. Wethertree, and I shall blow Sir Mortimer's brains out.

EFFIE. I—I was hasty this morning, Robert. I was so angry—I was very wrong to urge Sir Mortimer and Mr. Wethertree to——

SACK. (*aside*). Exactly—exactly—there it is—but she can't do it. I shall annihilate them both.

EFFIE. I—I came to your room, Robert—at the risk of my reputation—to—to——

SACK. Certainly. You came to my room at the risk of your reputation to save Sir Mortimer Muttonleg from personal danger. I shall carve Sir Mortimer Muttonleg joint from joint.

EFFIE (*coquettishly*). Sir Mortimer is such a delightful gentleman, you know.

SACK. (*aside*). I shall convert Sir Mortimer into Muttonleg pie.

EFFIE. But—I—I—wasn't thinking of Sir Mortimer Muttonleg.

SACK. Then I shall blow old Wethertree's brains out—if he has any.

EFFIE. I—I wasn't thinking of Sir Mortimer Muttonleg nor Mr. Wethertree either.

SACK. Oh!

EFFIE (*coquettishly*). I—I was thinking of—of—of the other one.

SACK. The—other—one.

EFFIE. Ahem—"Caterpillar!"

SACK. "Butterfly!" (*he opens his arms, she runs to him*). I have given up all the others—Virginia, Mrs. Alston, the stranger from Vermont. I have given them up with a jest—without a sigh—but when you came, Effie—I—I—I felt absolutely savage. I never knew how much I loved you until I thought you might love another. And now that you are really mine at last, I swear——

EFFIE. Nay—you have sworn too frequently already.

SACK. (*turning away*). True, Effie, you are right; an ever-changing, careless, reckless fellow like myself can never make you happy.

EFFIE. Per-haps—not—but—then—you—you might try, you know.

SACK. Yes—I will try, and now please let me swear—just once.

EFFIE. Well, then, you may swear once ; but, mind you, only once, for ever.

SACK. (*raising his hand*). Then I swear (*knock* L. 2. E.)—Damn that door !

EFFIE. Oh, somebody's coming ; if it should be father, he'd be in such a rage—or some other gentleman—conceal me somewhere (*runs* R. C.)—here.

SACK. No—there's a man in that room.

EFFIE. A man ! this closet, then (*runs to* C., *starts back at seeing opera cloak.* SACK. *picks it up and puts it up his back under his coat, leaving a portion seen*). An opera cloak ; oh ! Robert, Robert, is there a "*man*" in there, too. (*A knock* L. 2. E. *She runs to* L. C., *sees bonnet and starts back.*) Oh, Robert, Robert, did the "*man*" in there wear this (*he seizes it and puts it in the breast of his coat, and buttons coat over it. Rapid knock* L. 2. E.)

SACK. (*opening door*, R. C.). I'll explain all—in here (*aside*). Egad, I'd rather trust her reputation with Benedict than with another woman (*takes her hand and leads her to room* R. C.). There's no help for it, my darling, you must go into this room.

EFFIE (*pausing*). Oh Robert, Robert, if you are deceiving me again (*he hurries her in* R.).

[SACK. *shuts door,* R. C. *Knock* L. 2. E. SACK. *crosses to door.* BEN. *rushes from his room* R. C. *staring wildly.*

BEN. I say, Sackett, what in thunder—you've put a *woman* in my room !

SACK. Why, confound it, man, you're not afraid of a woman !

BEN. Ain't I ? What will the widow say ?

SICK. My dear fellow, I've chosen your room as a place of safety, for her reputation. I have the most implicit confidence in your honour.

BEN. (*taking* SACK.'s *hand*). My dear Sackett, you have more confidence in me than I have in myself.

[*Hurries out of door* R. C. *Rapid knock.*

SACK. (*opening door* L. 2. E.). Come in, sir.

Enter MRS. ALSTON *rapidly* ; SACK. *recoils as she enters. She drops lace shawl* L. C. *as she crosses* R.

SACK. Another woman !

MRS. ALSTON. Mr. Sackett, where's Mr. Benedict?

SACK. (*assuming a very serious air*). Alas! my dear Olivia, you are too late!

MRS. ALSTON. Too late—Oh! heaven! do not say that.

SACK. Jack was my friend—my schoolmate, the companion of my early years.

MRS. ALSTON. Surely you have not——

SACK. I urged him to reflect—to consider our relations—

MRS. ALSTON. You have not fought already.

SACK. Tears came into his eyes, he grasped me by the hand——

MRS. ALSTON. Oh, this suspense is terrible!

SACK. "Robert," said he, "we are old friends—but you have insulted the woman whom I love better than ten thousand lives"—I think it was ten thousand lives—I forget the exact number—"the woman whom I love better than ten thousand lives; she insists upon the satisfaction of a gentleman—I mean the satisfaction of a woman—and I shall protect her honour at the expense of friendship, life, everything that is dear to me." As we raised our pistols—

MRS. ALSTON. Oh heaven! as you raised your pistols——

SACK. As we raised our pistols, I said to him, "Benedict, my dear boy—it isn't too late yet;" but it was too late; his bullet whizzed past my ear, and landed in the wall beyond.

MRS. ALSTON. And your bullet?

SACK. My bullet missed my friend's heart—by less than eighteen inches. He fell; a surgeon was summoned, and he now lies in the next room in a delirious condition—a victim of his love for you, madam, and his devotion to the dictates of manly honour.

MRS. ALSTON. He lies in the next room?

SACK. He lies in the next room. (*aside*) and *I* lie in *this* room.

MRS. ALSTON. I will fly to him at once—I will—

[*Goes to door* R. C. SACK. *hurries and places himself between her and door.*

SACK. Not for the world, madam, not for the world—the surgeon is with him this very moment.

MRS. ALSTON. Oh, he would rather have me by his side than a thousand surgeons.

SACK. I dare say he would, Mrs. Alston; but the surgeon has given strict orders that *she*—I would say that *he*—must be entirely alone with Mr. Benedict.

MRS. ALSTON. Mr. Sackett, stand back; Mr. Benedict suffering on my account. I insist on flying to his side.

[*She pushes him aside ; flies to door ; opens it, and enters
R. C. SACK staggers to chair R. of table and sinks in it.*
SACK. Oh Lord, oh Lord, now for an explosion.
[*MRS. ALSTON screams within ; SACK. is lighting a cigar.
Re-enter MRS. ALSTON, followed by BEN., trying to explain ;
they walk R. and L. and up and down.*
BEN. My dear Olivia !——
MRS. ALSTON. Silence, sir, not a word from you ! Go back
to your surgeon, sir !
BEN. (R.). " Surgeon !"
MRS. ALSTON (L. *to* SACK., *who turns his back, striding his
chair, as she turns to him*). So this is your " delirium," sir—
a " victim of his love for me, and his devotion to the dictates
of manly honour !"—Oh ! I could tear his eyes out—and those
of his " surgeon " too.
BEN. " Surgeon !"
MRS. ALSTON (*to* BEN.). Never speak to me again !—never
dream of me—never come into my presence ! Go back to
your " surgeon."
BEN. " Surgeon !"
MRS. ALSTON. Go back to your " surgeon," sir !
[*She goes to L. 2. E., opening it suddenly. WETH. stumbles
in as if just knocking ; he falls in her arms, gathers himself
up. Exit MRS. ALSTON L. 2. E , angrily.*
WETH. (*confused*). I beg your pardon !
SACK. (*to* BEN.). Off with your dressing-gown, off with
your dressing-gown. Here's your coat, if you value the
widow's love—this is the critical moment—attack the enemy's
batteries— horse, foot, and artillery.
BEN. But, Sackett, I dare not face a woman—and particularly a widow—in such a condition as that.
SACK. Nonsense ! be a man. A woman in a passion is a
woman at her weakest moment. Confront her—meet her
face to face ; strike now or never ; the victory's yours.
BEN. (*hurrying*). I am leaping into the very jaw of death .
say a prayer for me, old boy.
[*He opens door L. 2. E. suddenly ; SIR MORT. stumbles in.
as if knocking. BEN. throws him across stage R. and
rushes out.*
SIR MORT. Beg pardon, sir.
SACK. (C.). Gentlemen, I've been waiting for you. It is
exactly twenty minutes before five ; don't apologise, however.
The coroners haven't arrived yet.
SIR MORT. Coroners !
SACK. I left word for a couple of coroners to drop in about
this time ; they are a little late—but it doesn't matter— the
corpses are not quite ready.

WETH. Corpses!

SACK. The undertaker will disappoint us, I fear. The coffins will be all right—two of them—with silver-plated handles.

SIR MORT. Coffins!—silver-plated handles!

SACK. But he has only one hearse to spare; do you object to riding double, gentlemen?

WETH. Riding double!

SIR MORT. Riding double!

[EFFIE *looks out, screams, and shuts door.* WETH. *and* SIR MORT. *start and stare* R. LUCY *looks from closet* C. WETH. *and* SIR MORT. *turn and stare up stage. All look round in amazement.*

SACK. Gentlemen, this is a very remarkable room; it is known as the Echo Chamber.

WETH. Those were very remarkable echoes.

SIR MORT. Those echoes do business apparently on their own responsibility; they are entirely independent of any original sound.

WETH. Mr. Sackett. I called at your room at the appointed hour. in the hope that we might arrange our difficulties upon a mutually satisfactory basis.

SIR MORT. Exactly the same with myself; the relations which Miss Remington bears towards me——

WETH. (*sharply*). Miss Remington don't bear any relations towards you at all, sir!

SIR MORT. I beg your pardon. Miss Remington consented to be the wife of my bosom, the day before yesterday afternoon.

WETH. I beg *your* pardon; you are mistaken in the bosom, Sir Mortimer. Miss Remington consented to be the wife of *my* bosom.

SIR MORT. My dear fellow—it was my bosom, I assure you.

WETH. My bosom, I will swear.

SACK. Ah, gentlemen, let us settle the matter at once; how lucky it is that I have the weapons at hand. Here is something for each of your bosoms. Here you are, Mr. Wethertree—here you are, Sir Mortimer (*hands them pistols*). No preliminaries are necessary. One of these pistols is loaded with ball, the other is not. You will take your place there, Mr. Wethertree. Sir Mortimer, you will stand there. You settle with each other, and I will settle with the sur- vivor.   [*Scream.*

LUCY, EFFIE, and VIRGINIA (*peeping out*). Oh! they're going to fight. Ah! (*together*).   [*A knock.*

Enter LITTLEFIELD.

LITTLEFIELD. Sorry to have detained you, Mr. Sackett, I was unexpectedly detained.

Enter MAJOR, L. 2. E.

MAJOR. Better late than never, my dear Sackett. Ah! you have not forgotten the wine, I see.

[*Goes to* R. *of table and pours out wine.*

Enter CARTER *and* FREDERICK, *with pistol-case*, L. 2. E.

CARTER (L. C.). Open the box, Frederick. I am not too late, I see. Mr. Sackett, you are prepared, I suppose, to give me the satisfaction of a gentleman.

Enter GYP, *followed by* MR. *and* MRS VAN. *and old* REM.

GYP. Heah dey is, gemmen, pistols and cigars. I know'd suffin was up.

VAN. (L. C.). Mr. Sackett, Carter, Sir Mortimer, Major, Mr. Wethertree, Littlefield.

MRS. VAN. (*on opening box*). Ah! pistols—more pistols. Gentlemen, what does this mean?

[VAN. *sees shawl dropped by* MRS. ALSTON.

VAN. (*picking up shawl*). Eh, what (*looks all round*). This doesn't belong to any of you gentlemen, I suppose?

[*All stare at shawl, then at* SACK.

MRS. VAN. A lady's shawl in Mr. Sackett's private apartment. I am positively shocked.

OLD REM. M'm, so am I.

WETH. It doesn't belong to me.

SIR MORT. Nor to me.

SACK. Eh! oh—a shawl; that's very odd. How did I happen to leave that shawl in this room?

VAN. M'm, I'm not quite certain that *you* did leave it in this room.

OLD REM. (L.). I think myself there is some doubt on that point.

SACK. (C.). That shawl is one of the most valuable memen-toes in my possession.

VAN. Ah!

OLD REM. M'm.

SACK. I wouldn't lose that shawl for the world.

VAN. Oh, I dare say not.

SACK. I—I often take that shawl out of my trunk when I am alone, and no one by to interrupt the sweet memories which float into my brain. I unfold that shawl with all the tenderness of early manhood, and as I contemplate its folds

I think of her whose shoulders it once adorned. My poor old aunt! (*He walks* R.)

SIM. M. Ahem!

OLD REM. Gammon!

CARTER. Stuff and nonsense } *together.*
WETH. Very likely

[*The three old gentlemen punching each other in the ribs,* L. C.]

VAN. M'm—y-e-s—he—he—he—it belonged to his aunt.

FRED. I notice I'd like an aunt or two of the same kind.

MAJOR (*at back of table—raising glass*). Gentlemen, here's a glass to the memory of Mr. Sackett's aunt.

WETH. (*to* SIR M.). I say, Sir Mortimer, the shawl belongs to one of those echoes.

[SACKETT *sees* EFFIE'S *scarf, snatches it up, and crams it into his coat-tail pocket, leaving part exposed, just in time to escape detection as they all turn to him. He walks* C.

SACK. When I was a very little boy——

CARTER. When they called you Bob for short.

SACK. Yes, my aunt always called me "Bob." I was left an orphan when I was a very little boy. My aunt was more than a mother to me; I was left in her care. She brought me up.

VAN. M'm, I can't say much for the way she did it.

SACK. (C.). I remember one day, when I was a very little boy, my aunt laid her hand upon me.

OLD REM. M'm, I don't think your aunt laid her hand upon you quite often enough when you were a little boy.

SACK. Oh, yes, she did. I shall never forget that woman as long as I live. I shall never forget her as long as I have any feeling in my heart, or in any other part of my body. (*Walks* L., *the old gents together laughing as before.*)

OLD REM. Ha—ha. I say–if he'd only had six or eight more aunts when he was a very little boy.

VAN. And if they'd all have laid their slippers on him in stead of their hands.

CARTER. Egad, he wouldn't be so partial to the female sex and other people's wives.

SACK. (C.). Gentlemen, it may be a laughing matter to you; but I assure you, gentlemen, my early memories of my aunt are no laughing matter to me.

ALL. Ha—ha—ha (*punching each other all round*).

SACK. Gentlemen, there are moments in every man's life when the recollections of the past come floating upon the memory like aromatic zephyrs from a distant land—

moments, gentlemen, when one wishes to be alone (*significantly*).

ALL. Ahem!

SACK. When one *longs* to be alone.

ALL (*aside*). Yes,—very likely.

SACK. There are moments, gentlemen, when the heart comes swelling into the throat——

VAN. I should say there were moments also when it came swelling into the back. (*Rubs his hand over the back of his coat.*)

SACK. Sir!

OLD REM. (*crossing to* L. C.). You have a remarkably fine figure, Mr. Sackett.

SACK. Oh, you like my figure. Yes, I always did pride myself on my figure.

[VANDERPOOL *pulls opera-cloak from under his coat, looks at it as the conversation proceeds; then throws it over his arm.*

MRS. V. (R. *of* SACKETT). I beg your pardon, Mr. Sackett. (*She pulls a bonnet string which brings* VIRG.'s *bonnet from his breast.*) Did this also belong to your aunt?

SACK. That! eh! oh, no! That belonged to my sister; she was the only sister I ever had, Mrs. Vanderpool. (*As he speaks* OLD REM. *pulls* EFFIE'S *scarf from his coat-tail pocket.*)

OLD REM. Did this belong to your sister also, Mr. Sackett?

SACK. (*turning to him*). Eh! That, oh, ahem! No—that belonged to another sister.

MRS. V. Another sister! I thought this was the only sister you ever had.

SACK. Oh, yes, certainly that was the only sister *I* ever had. This belonged to another man's sister.

VAN. Egad, I suspected as much!

CARTER. I could swear they *all* belonged to "another man's sister."

MAJOR (*at table*). Here's the very good health of "another man's sister."

MRS. VAN. (*starting, looking at bonnet*). Ah! Virginia! and it's Virginia's bonnet! Where's her head?

VAN. Eh? What? (*Starts up with her, dropping opera-cloak.*)

OLD REM. (*crosses to* R.). Egad, this is Effie's white lace scarf.

CARTER (*taking up opera-cloak*). Eh?—what?—Mrs. Carter's opera-cloak?

VS 7 7.

[CARTER *opens wardrobe* C.　MRS. VAN. *opens door* L.
　　REM. *opens door* R. *Scream from all the young women.*
CARTER (R. C.). Mrs. Carter herself !
OLD REM. (R. C.). They call this travelling for pleasure !
LITT. *and* MAJOR. Virginia Vanderpool !
SIR M. Effie Remington, by Jove !
LUCY *coming* C., *her head down, she leans against chair* C.
　　EFFIE *and* VIRG., R. *and* L., *confused.*
SACK. My friends, I—I dare say you—you are somewhat
surprised at——
OLD REM. M'm, yes, somewhat.
SACK. The ladies—Mrs. Carter, Miss Vanderpool, Miss
Remington—the ladies—in fact, before the gentlemen ar-
rived, the ladies all entered this apartment—together.
EFFIE, VIRG., *and* LUCY. Oh, yes,—we all came in
together.
SACK. They all came in together to intercede with me for
those they love best, to save them from the certain destruc-
tion which awaited them at my hands. Miss Virginia ex-
claimed to me—" Oh, Robert, you will not meet Frank
Littlefield ; you will not risk a life that has become so dear
to me. I have learned to love Frank Littlefield."
VAN. Ah ! ahem !
LITTLEFIELD. My dear Virginia.
VIRG. Frank (*crosses to him*).
SACK. Take her, Littlefield ; make her happy.　I give
you both my blessing.　I'll be your brother-in-law.　(*Turns
to* CARTER) Mr. Carter, I owe you an apology and an explanation.　Mrs. Carter entered my room to-day to plead
for your safety only.　(*Takes* LUCY's *hand*) Take her, Carter,
in all her blushing loveliness (*passes her to* CARTER—FRED
receives her).
CARTER. Devil take that boy.　(LUCY *slaps* FRED, *and
runs to* CARTER.)
SACK. (*coming* L. C.). Ahem ! Miss Effie.
EFFIE (R. C.). Ahem ! Robert,—you may ask papa.
SACK. My dear Mr. Remington——
OLD REM. (R. C.). I think it's rather late in the day to
ask papa.　(EFFIE *and* SACK *embrace.*)
WETH. (R.). Ahem, I say, Sir Mortimer, there are as good
fish in the sea as ever was caught (*goes up*).
SIR M. (R.). I don't think I'll fish any more in American
waters.　These American girls are the most unaccountable
creatures.
Enter BEN. *and* MRS. A. *arm in arm,* L. 2 C. BEN.
　　　　　leading her L. C.
SACK. Hallo ! an unconditional surrender.

BEN. (L. C.). Certainly ; that is the regular thing, Bob.

MRS. A. What could I do ? The man was perfectly out-
rageous. The more I silenced him the more he talked. I
capitulated for the sake of peace. I have exacted one condition, however. Whenever he needs a "surgeon" again,
he must call on me. Oh, here is my lace shawl. I was
wondering where I left it. (*Takes shawl from* VAN.'s *arm.
Sensation.*)

VAN. Ah—then you are Mr. Sackett's aunt.

OLD R. Egad, all the women in the house have been here.

MRS. A. Mr. Sackett's aunt !

CARTER. You were more than a mother to him.

MRS. A I—more than a mother to Mr. Sackett !—I've
never been anything of the kind to anybody.

SACK. But here's a little woman, who *will* be more than a
mother to me—more than a sister—brother—cousin—uncle—
aunt—more than a mother-in-law—more than all the world
beside—my wife. (*To audience*) Ladies and gentlemen—
when I was a very little boy——

EFFIE. There—never mind when you were a very little
boy——

SACK. Young gentlemen, whenever you find a lady in
your arms or your heart——

EFFIE. Allow her to "remain in the place in which she
originally fell."

CURTAIN.